# A HOOD
# *Princess*

*An Eastside Love Story*

A NOVEL BY
# K.A. WILLIAMS

© *2019 Royalty Publishing House*

**Published by Royalty Publishing House**
*www.royaltypublishinghouse.com*

**ALL RIGHTS RESERVED**
Any unauthorized reprint or use of the material is prohibited. No part of this book may be reproduced or transmitted in any form or by any means, electronic or mechanical, including photocopying, recording, or by any information storage without express permission by the author or publisher. This is an original work of fiction. Names, characters, places and incidents are either products of the author's imagination or are used fictitiously and any resemblance to actual persons, living or dead, is entirely coincidental.
**Contains explicit language & adult themes suitable for ages 16+ only.**

**Royalty Publishing House** is now accepting manuscripts from aspiring or experienced urban romance authors!

## WHAT MAY PLACE YOU ABOVE THE REST:

Heroes who are the ultimate book bae: strong-willed, maybe a little rough around the edges but willing to risk it all for the woman he loves.

Heroines who are the ultimate match: the girl next door type, not perfect - has her faults but is still a decent person. One who is willing to risk it all for the man she loves.

The rest is up to you! Just be creative, think out of the box, keep it sexy and intriguing!

If you'd like to join the Royal family, send us the first 15K words (60 pages) of your completed manuscript to submissions@royaltypublishinghouse.com

# SYNOPSIS

*S*ome hoods are violent, and will play you out of your shoes, while others are just underprivileged suburbs, and everybody on the block is one big family...

Daughter of the Eastside Warriors' honcho, eighteen-year-old Lyric has a dream of making it out of the hood and away from her father's dynasty by performing her way into the limelight as a rapper. And, with the help of her producer boyfriend by the name of Beatz, she's well on her way to fulfilling her dreams with love guiding their steps.

However, some dreams aren't meant to be fulfilled, and not all love lasts. Lyric learns firsthand when tragedy strikes, forcing her to put her dreams on hold while falling into the arms of her father's right-hand man, Osiris.

While torn between two worlds, Lyric finds herself in a love affair with her first love and the man who signed his name in blood to protect her.

# PROLOGUE

*O*ne to the right, three to the left. Four to the right, one to the left.

*This shit is crazy,* Don thought as he struggled to open the safe. As the honcho of the Eastside Warriors, with over twenty years under his belt, he never ran into a situation that was beyond his control.

With about ten Warriors standing behind him, Don continued to mess around with the safe. His team had his back. He didn't have to worry about somebody trying to come up and sneak him. They stayed on their tens.

*Maybe he said,* one to the left, three to the right. Four to the left, one to the right. After putting the combination in for a second time, the safe opened at Don's request. His eyes fell upon at least one million dollars with diamonds sitting pretty in a plastic Ziploc bag on top of the stacks.

"Bag all this shit up. I told that nigga not to mess with me," Don ordered the ten Warriors. They followed his request without breathing hesitation. They knew better than to even look like they wanted to question him. The men who were by his side since the nineties knew what he did to muthafuckas who failed to follow the rules.

"That nigga did dirt under the table with my foes while I housed alliance with his crew. Well, today the nigga gets banished from the streets." Don strolled out the house with Gates. Gates was Don's right hand in rank. He was initiated into the crew three short years back. He was a nigga from South Louisiana. He threw around the slang word *whoadie* more than Don liked, but he was loyal to the team. He showed Don that he was down, and has been riding ever since. So, Don overlooked his minor dislikes of the nigga's word usage and viewed him as a loyal Warrior who had potential.

"What ya want us to do with the nigga?" Gates waved a Glock 19 9mm around like he was ready to spray a nigga. "You said the nigga being banished from the streets, so let me get him, whoadie. C'mon big dawg, I call dibs on the hoe ass nigga."

"Naw, I got this." Don fired up a nice blunt of Kush. Although he stayed on high alert, he took the edge off once in a while. Dealing with all the shit he had going on, any nigga would be in desperate need of a minor escape. "My face has to be the last one he sees before I hand him that one-way ticket out."

On beat, the crew walked out the house loaded with cash tucked away in duffel bags. The code had always been to never take from a crew that's in alliance with another crew, but Don dropped the 211 Vipers from under his wings. He dropped their ass and took whatever money he loaned over the years. It was their way of getting out of his debt without him having to blow a hole through each of their heads.

"Gates, Ken, Dre, I need y'all to dip with me. The rest of you, go take this money and stash it at HQ." Don hopped in the back of the all-white Cadillac Escalade without any further words. They were given orders and that was final. Don wasn't the kind of man to do a whole lot of talking. When he meant business, they knew what was up.

\* \* \*

*I told this nigga not to fuck with me.* Don entered the room where they held the honcho of 211 Vipers hostage. When the Eastside Warriors and 211 Vipers made their alliance in stone, the OG Cappo was still sitting on the throne ruling the crew with a horsewhip. Cappo never played about breaking the code; he offed niggas without a word for placing his team in danger. Things changed when he died and his nephew, Gooch took over. He refused to pay homage to Don, or to follow the rules that were written before he was old enough to wipe his ass.

Out of respect to Cappo's legacy, Don stuck it out with the 211 Vipers. He and Cappo went way back. They swore their alliance when they both were young niggas in the game; before their names blew across the states as muthafuckin' honchos.

"Cappo would be disappointed in the shit you do on his stomping grounds. I let you slide too many times due to your uncle's legacy. I see now, I made a mistake. I should've banished your ass when you first decided to fuckin' cross me." Don retrieved the gold AK-47. There were fancier guns out there, but he chose to stick with what he knew could fuck a nigga up in a few seconds. The AK was given to him decades ago when he first sealed his name in blood on the streets. He made a few adjustments to it over the years and made it shoot like new. "Nigga you crossed a real OG out here. You swore alliance with the crew that wants my ass dead."

"Man, fuck you nigga. You think my niggas just gon' bow to your feet when you off me? Naw, my homies gon' ride for me. 211 'til all our fuckin caskets drop. You old niggas don't like change, and that's why so many new gangs thriving. It's about change nigga." Gooch shot his words at Don like a real savage. It wasn't any bitch in his blood. Although he did shit his uncle wouldn't be proud of, he still housed one value: to never bow to any nigga's feet that you don't respect.

"I'm all about change young homie, but all change ain't a good change. You making peace with niggas who will off you and every nigga in partnership with you. The Serge G's ain't for nobody but themselves. They swear alliance with you one day then cut your throat the next. You sold me out, nigga; all of us out." Don gave Gates a silent order that the two of them could only understand. Gates moved across the room over to Don. He untied the blindfold from Gooch's eyes. Whenever Don banished a nigga from the streets, he favored granting their ticket through execution shooting, body tied to a pole while they waited to meet their maker.

"Tell Cappo I said what's up." Don pulled the trigger as a calmness washed over his body. He didn't let up on the trigger until the banana clip emptied.

# OSIRIS

"I want you to cut that nigga open." Don shot his demands at me. Being with the Eastside Warriors put food on the table and made sure the bills were paid. The things Don did to save me over a decade ago would put anyone in debt for a lifetime. The nigga was like Black Jesus walking to most everybody in the hood we both represented. Over the years, I watched Don every step of the way. I wanted to be like him. He was great at what he did. His enemies never could dig the way his heart bent towards the hood. That was Don's thing; his choices, the way he chose to do business, it all reflected on his love for the hood. You must respect a man like that.

"Please, man. I was just trying to make a little extra on the side for my daughter's birthday. You have children right?" Ken pled for his life. I couldn't feel sorry for a man like that. He knew the consequences of his actions. The nigga had to pay his dues.

"Yeah, I have children, but I bust my ass every day to make sure food is on the table, food in their mouth along with clothes on their back. I never had to steal from a nigga to do that." Don took a gulp out of the Remy Martin bottle as he took a seat at least ten feet across the room to give me some space to do what had to be done.

"The worse thing, aside from betrayal, is theft. You stole from the man that helped you when everyone else turned their backs on you and counted you out," I said, revealing the samurai as fear crept in Ken's eyes. "You're a disgrace to the streets. You already know what happens to niggas who break the code, so you shouldn't act surprised." Niggas like Ken pissed me off. They betray the code of the streets like nothing would happen to them. They walk around for weeks, sometimes months at a time, like people forgot about their treason.

"Damn, you might as well kiss the nigga. Go ahead and slice him open." Don capped off the whiskey with his patience wearing thin.

I drew my arm back, brought it forward and allowed the sword to connect to Ken's stomach. The floor caught all the organs that fell out of his stomach. It was a beautiful sight. I always felt good whenever I could come through for the boss. "Now that's a lot of blood." According to my calculations, I been on Don's team for almost a decade. I did the cruelest things to put fear in another man's heart. None of it made me wince. I still slept like a baby at night without any of it bothering me. That's why Don pulled to me the way he did. He trusted me more than anybody else on the team.

Don clapped his hands. "That's what the fuck I'm talking about. I know you like letting the niggas know the wrong they've done, but that's how you fucking do it. You slice them in the middle of them trying to summon words."

I handed the sword over to my right hand, Trever. I walked out of the office to allow him to clean up the mess. Don was right behind me. Since earlier in the day, Don told me there was serious business to discuss with the new plans he had concerning the company. And I was anxious to get the conversation over with.

I fired up a blunt, waiting for Don to get on with the discussion. He knew my nerves were always shot whenever there was something serious on the table up for discussion.

"I been in this gang for a long time. I been running these streets for twenty plus years and I'm ready to turn it over." Don accepted the blunt I passed to him. On any other day, my blunt was never passed around. "I put you in charge of showing Lyric the game. I could do it myself, but you know I don't have that kind of time right now. With me trying to retire and shit, it comes with a lot of loose ends I need to tie up."

"I'm all for it. I think she'll be a helluva boss once she learns all the outs and ins. I wouldn't mind teaching her everything and serving as her right-hand as well. You sure that's what she wants to do?" I replied without giving my words much thought.

"She doesn't have a choice but to do as she's told. When a king dies or steps down, his children is next in line for the throne. Well, this is my empire and it follows my name, so she will be carrying out my duties as I see fit." Don passed the blunt back to me.

I couldn't stop thinking about how Lyric was going to take the news. We have never been in each other's company, exclusively, but I could always make observations. Lyric didn't seem like the type of girl who wanted to be involved with Don's empire. Just off street gossip, I knew she was ready for the day that she could up and leave without having anything to do with their family's business. Don's legacy.

"Not only do I want you to be her right hand when the time comes, but I also want you to stand by her side as her husband. I always wanted a strong man to be my son-in-law. Somebody that knows the business and I can trust. Plus, I see the way you look at her now." Don laid it all out there on me. Being married to Lyric would've been a dream come true. Since she was Don's daughter, I knew she wasn't like the bitches out there on the streets who hop from dick to dick. Naw, shawty was different; there was no choice but for her to be different.

"Damn, boss. I never would've expected this to come from you. She's a jewel and for you to trust me with her is beyond a blessing. I won't disappoint you." I took a few puffs of the blunt before putting it out. With Don's blessing, all I had to do was somehow convince Lyric that I was the better man for her. After a little while of observing her, I knew who she was cool with and what nigga was close enough to receive a chance with her. I had to make sure I made my move count.

Reaching out to shake my hand Don said, "I know you won't."

* * *

"So, you mean to tell me Don gave you his blessing to be with Lyric? Do you know how many niggas would beat your ass for that position?" Jab sat on the porch blazing. Whenever he and I were kicking it, we blazed while shooting dice and having deep conversations. Being first cousins only made our bond tighter over the years. The nigga was like my brother.

"Yeah, he's turning the company over to her and I'll be serving as her right hand. Then when the time is right, the plan is to be her husband." I shook the dice around in my left hand. I tossed them on the porch, praying like hell I hit a seven.

"Nigga you keep hitting like that you're gonna be paying up some big bucks." Jab picked up the dice from the porch. He played dice around the hood like it was a sport and he was trying to go to the playoffs. "You know if you fuck up, Don is going to fuck you up."

"Just like I told him, I'm not going to mess it up. I'll make sure she's protected and happy," I replied out of confidence. I slept with a lot of women. Word on the street, I even had a child on the way. If the bitch never stepped forward, it didn't count. With all the fucked up decisions and slutty ass females I boned, I was going to be a different man for Lyric. Change my entire outlook on women.

"I hear you bruh." Jab shook the dice again. He tossed them on the porch, and once they hit the scuffed ply board, he jumped up and hit me on the shoulder. "Pay up nigga!"

Already retrieving five twenties from my wallet, I replied, "Alright, alright. You got that."

"Damn right." Jab tucked the twenties away in his socks.

"You want to hit the scene with me tonight? Don is going out of town and I need to keep tabs on Lyric. She's going to be my real headache soon anyway, I might as well get a head start," I said.

"Yeah, I'll tag along." Jab agreed.

"Alright, I'll stop back by to scoop you up, bruh. And next time, we ain't playing with your rigged ass dice." I dipped off the porch. My house was right up the street from where Jab stayed. Well, my Mom Duke's house. With all the bread I was making, it was easy to snatch up a place to stay, but it was something about being close to my Mom Duke that ensured me she was safe. Leaving the nest hadn't ever been a big goal of mine, because I was too damn busy trying to pay her back for all she did for me. It was my turn to take care of her before it really was time for my ass to move out. At twenty-seven, I definitely wasn't getting any younger; the years was moving up on my ass.

"Aye ma, I'm going out later. I need you to make sure you keep these doors locked." I strolled down the only hallway in the house leading to her room. The house wasn't big, and at one time or another, it housed me and three of my siblings. Sharing a bedroom with them back then didn't give any of us the privacy we wanted. Those years are gone, and though sometimes I reminisced, I didn't like thinking about it for too long. We went through some rough shit back then. Shit that I tried to forget.

"Keep your voice down," Mom Duke murmured.

Pushing my hands forward, I opened the door to her room. It was around five in the evening, and usually, she would be in the kitchen whipping up dinner or on the porch playing cards with her friends. I never knew her to be cooped up in the room.

"You straight?" I walked inside of the room to see what she had going on.

"Well." Mom Duke sat upright on the bed. It looked like somebody had run her over with a truck and left her for dead. "I'm just in a lot of pain. My right breast is swollen and leaking. I don't what's wrong and I feel so tired."

"Do you need me to take you to the hospital? We can go right now. You know there's nothing that I have going on that comes before you." I took a seat on the side of the bed. Mom Duke was my backbone, and the thought of something happening to her made a lump of sadness form in my throat. My entire body went numb sitting there next to her.

"I already made an appointment to see my doctor tomorrow. I'll be fine. There's nothing the good Lord can't see me through. Go enjoy your Sunday night like you always do. Don't worry 'bout me." She reached for my hand and gave it a squeeze. I was sitting there not sure what to do when she had already told me what to do. Hell, what can a person do when the woman who birthed them was suffering from an agonizing pain that was too stubborn to subside?

# BEATZ

The beat was blasting through the studio headphones. Music is what kept my mind sane, and if I kept chasing after my dreams, it would be music that got my ass out the hood. I saw too many men fall by the wayside of gang violence. God being the director of my life, I would rise above the environment that so many were accustomed to.

Removing the headphones from my ears to see what noise I heard outside, my head was slammed against the walnut desk.

*BOOP!*

"See baby savage, it's not safe out here if you don't have a set that you rep." T-Max's voice blared around the small studio. I never had to see anyone's face to know their voice. Then on the flip, T-Max was always running up on me trying to put fear in my heart in hopes that I surrendered to the little power that 211 Vipers still possessed after my first cousin, Gooch, was murdered. He was the honcho after our uncle Cappo lost the fight to sudden sickness. The streets never could off him, but God; He was the real thug. He took niggas whenever he pleased.

T-Max forced my head up, and when he did, my eyes were looking into the barrel of an AR-15. "I would blow a hole right through your skull, but if you rep 211 with your entire life can't any nigga fuck with you."

"You might as well kill me then because I'm not getting mixed up in street malice. Aren't you tired of throwing up sets, slanging dope, and dropping niggas?" Anybody standing in the room would get the impression that I wasn't afraid of shit, but my heart was beating at the speed of lightning. My uncle was dead, and Gooch was dead. The 211s could've done whatever they wanted to me.

"Your uncle ruled, Gooch ruled, why won't you step up to claim the throne, baby savage? Not living up to the family's name is disrespecting the niggas who died for this shit. And Gooch… Don did him dirty. We have to make our army grow if we want to put a bullet through his existence." T-Max lowered the gun. He strolled around the studio as best as the small space allowed, and I was finally able to look around the place. For a moment, I thought T-Max rode up on the Eastside without protection, but I heard his goons speaking in code outside the studio.

"You can still do your rapping shit and be honcho of the 211s. It's in your blood." T-Max was set on changing my mind. Since turning eighteen the year before, he was persistent with his approach on recruiting me. It wasn't for some low-rank position either; he was trying to force me to wear the same title as my two kinsmen before me. Muthafuckin' *honcho*.

"You been rolling with the 211 Vipers since my uncle ran it with Thor's hammer, so why the fuck won't you step up? You served as uncle Cappo's right hand, and was third in rank when Gooch took over." T-Max acted like a young nigga, he wasn't though. T-Max easily pushed his early forties. He messed with young girls like he was still a teenager and dressed down to the T like no other in town. He was sharp; a little more feared than most, too.

"And you talking about something that happened thirteen years ago.

Let that shit go." I raised from the chair after I built the small nerves I had up.

"Yeah, I heard 'bout you. Falling under the spell of Don's oldest daughter. Is that why you won't step up? Because you'll be her old man's foe? I don't know where you been, but family comes before anybody, and if the shoe was on the other foot, Gooch would've been riding for you until your enemies paid the highest price." T-Max raised the AR-15 at me again like he was in contemplation to murder me or let me walk like all the other times I turned down ruling the 211s.

"Yeah, I been with the 211s since you were in diapers, but that don't mean I have the right to step up as honcho. The Alejos name is speared in blood over the 211s, they will respect you more than anybody claim as honcho." T-Max held a clear aim on me as my heart dropped to my boxers. He showed me time and time again, that it was he who had mercy on my life, and it was he who could blast my ass in my own studio. "We making a hit on Don's new recruit tonight, making it look like a legit tragedy. So, my hands are tied, but you have until the end of the week to make your decision."

T-Max made it clear that he and the Eastside Warriors weren't ever going to eat at the same table as brothers. He was set on beef that happened when I was six. He made it seem like I knew Gooch, as if the nigga brought me up from a lil' savage. I didn't owe any dead honcho my life. What happened thirteen years ago happened. Plus, he was right; I was rolling with Don's daughter, Lyric. We been close friends since the sandbox in kindergarten, and just a month ago things turned serious between us.

* * *

Lyric laid on the couch with her legs crossed. It was like magic whenever we were together, and just like me, she didn't want anything to do with the streets. We had dreams bigger than gangs, throwing up sets and selling dope to any and everybody who had the money to buy.

"You just going to sit at that desk all night?" Since we fooled around for the first time a month ago, I peeped how her voice changed whenever she was in the mood to have me in all the ways only she could imagine.

"Hold on; this dope ass hook just popped up out of nowhere. I think this will make a sick song." I bopped my head to the beat like I did seven days per week. Music was my lifeline. "Man, you gon' like this joint once I put it all together."

"Is that so?" Lyric placed her hands on my shoulders, allowing them to travel to my chest. A few years back I didn't look at her as a girlfriend or anything close. She was literally my best friend. When you grow up with somebody, it's hard to look at them in another light. The cosmos shifted for us though, and took us both by surprise.

"Yeah." I closed my eyes for a second, trying to make my dick stay tamed. I wanted her more than she would ever know; I just didn't want her to think I was an amateur at it. So, I made it seem like the smallest things didn't make my dick beat against my pants in an attempt to be set free.

"Well, that can wait. I want all of your attention, babe." Lyric's voice hung in the air like a beautiful harmony. She made my back hairs stand up like they possessed their own pair of legs.

The whole time she was there, I was out of my element. T-Max had just left from trying to get me drafted as the honcho of 211 Vipers. Of all the people, I knew Lyric would be the first one to give ear to my words, but her dad was the honcho of the Warriors. I couldn't just tell her the 211s were trying to draft me in. Those were the last words that I needed Don to hear. He already wasn't fond of me, and the reason being was that Alejos' blood made up half of my genetic makeup. He cut ties with the 211s thirteen years ago and counted everybody in association with them an enemy. I wasn't though. I wasn't an enemy to anybody. Never had a reason to hate another person.

I knew if Lyric found out about my people, well, that the people my family had ties with was an enemy to her, she wouldn't look at me the same. She was going to honor Don's wish to leave me alone.

"Alright, you can have all that." I placed the headphones on the desk and twirled the chair around so that I was facing Lyric. With her hands traveling back to my shoulders, I grabbed as much ass as my hands allowed. Lyric had cake for days with a snatched waistline to match. She was bad without anyone having to put it in her head.

"Good." Lyric crossed her legs over me and sat on my lap to face me. She gave me bird peck kisses before she snaked her tongue in my mouth like a pro. As close friends, I never heard her mention any nigga being with her. A month before that night, I knew for a fact I was the first nigga to hit it, however, she took control like she was a pro. Her kisses would send any man into cardiac arrest if he wasn't able to hit after. "My pussy is flowing like a river in my underwear. Do you want to feel?"

"Uhm, yeah." I let the words out as best as I could through tongue kissing, I unbuckled her stone washed jeans and slipped my hands down to her sex. Lyric was going to drive me crazy with what she was doing to me. I had only been with two girls before her. The other I was still with, but I was trying to come up with an excuse to drop her since Lyric and I were more than friends now.

"You feel how wet I am?" Lyric removed her mouth from mine and travel from my face to my ear with her tongue. I couldn't take her teasing me anymore, so I stood up with her legs wrapped around me. I carried her a foot across the room and lowered her onto the couch. Then I quickly made my way over to the door to lock it. Any time she told me she was coming over, I made sure to have a condom in my possession.

When I made it back over to the couch, she was already naked playing with the hood of her pussy. I slipped out of my clothes without hesitation. I joined her on the couch. Her legs were spread apart, waiting for me to enter her with my hard on.

*She gon' make me crazy, mopping savages with the floor about her,* I thought as I allowed her to guide my dick in her deep. Lyric wasn't the kind of woman to always force a man to take control; she enjoyed being in control of situations sometimes, which I didn't mind one bit.

"Mmmmm." Lyric licked her fingers after my dick was inserted. The view of her almost made me bust a nut before I even started to thrust. It felt like her pussy sucked me into a tight hold and refused to release me. I thrust quick and deep. She gripped my ass and almost made me jump out my flesh. She did it so she could make me slow down my strokes. Whenever I got too excited, she let me know by catching me off guard with some shit like that.

"You gon' learn everything isn't to be rushed." Lyric grinded her hips to meet my now slow, deep thrusts. Our bodies were in sync, almost like our souls were one. As we made love without a beat of music, our bodies made their own song. However, even in the moment of having the best sex I ever had, I was stuck with the thought of me kind of betraying her 'bout not telling her what was going on out there. About the hit T-Max and the 211s were about to do to one of Don's new recruits.

# LYRIC

"I know that ain't the little Lyric that's supposed to be at home before the streetlights come on." I turned around time I heard Osiris's voice. He was a friend of the family, closer to my pop than anyone. That still didn't stop him from having eyes for me. He never really came out and told me he wanted me to ride with him like that; I just knew. The way he looked at me whenever he was at the house kicking it with my pop, gave his thoughts away every damn time.

"Shit," I blurted out. On the weekends, I was always sneaking out the house because Pop was gone on business trips and my momma slept hard as fuck. I knew whenever one of the family's guards rode around the block to come check our property, per Pop's wish, while he was away. I would leave out the house right after he was done making sure nobody was trying to break in to harm us.

"What?" Beatz was at least five steps ahead of me.

"He's ranked as the right hand for the Eastside Warriors, like really close friends with my pop," I replied in a hushed tone.

"Come here real quick," Osiris said from his blue 1971 Plymouth

Barracuda. He was a sucker for classic cars like my pop, which made me throw up in my mouth every time. The last thing I needed in my life was another man trying to cripple my every damn move. "Did you hear me?"

"I'm coming, damn!" I fussed. Although Beatz didn't know too much about Osiris, I figured Osiris knew all there was to know about Beatz, because my pop made sure he and his crew kept close tabs on the people I hung out with. I couldn't fucking breathe without one of his minions being in my muthafuckin' business.

When I turned my attention back to Beatz, it was hard for me to even look at him straight. That Friday night was supposed to be for us to really kick it. On regular days, I had my own little stuff going on while he was busy in the studio trying to be the next Jay Z. It was sometimes impossible to make time for each other, but we owed ourselves that night. Our relationship longed for a night like that; just the two of us out on the town living like actual youths for a change.

"I'm sorry, I gotta go." I finally allowed the words to slip out.

"It's cool, I understand all that. Just hit me up whenever you want to hang out or make some hits in the studio. You have some talent that needs to be heard, but on top of all that, you know I can't be away from you for long." Beatz walked up to me and gave me a hug. His hugs always made me feel ten times better. He was my nigga even with our relationship still being a secret to the streets. He still had a girl he had to cut loose and all that, while I had a pop who despised him, so neither of us was in favor of going public just yet. "I will," I replied as I slowly released Beatz.

I headed across the parking lot to Osiris ready to snap him up. He worked for Pop, and his loyalty was with our family. He was doing his job and I understood that, but damn the shit got old.

"You acting like I'm bugging or some." Osiris licked his top lip. He leaned against his car like he was the coolest nigga walking the streets, and I had to give it to him; he was all that and a bag of chips.

"Are you going to tell or what?" I looked right into Osiris's eyes. He had the fucking nerves to smile at me the way he did.

"I really should, especially since you were out here with that goofy ass nigga. What can he even do for you, Lyric? How can somebody like that even protect you?" Osiris shook his head. "You know what, naw I'm not gonna tell because clearly what you do isn't none of my fuckin' business."

"Well, I'm happy you finally realize that." I walked away from Osiris with the same attitude I approached him with.

"I'm not done talking to you." Osiris snatched me back to him. He knew he was all out of line even touching me because if my pop found out, he would've made sure Osiris lost the same hand he touched his daughter with.

"Let go of me. I'm not your girl or anything like that, so don't push all up on me." I snapped harder than I intended to. Osiris was only trying to look out for me; I understood that. It was part of his job, due to the contract he and Pop shared. With me knowing the facts, it still never stopped me from losing my temper.

"Alright." Osiris released the grip he had on my arm. "You know Mansfield is a small town and if anybody from the Eastside or wherever see you out here, they will rat you the fuck out. And you know you don't suppose to be out here making your dad's name look bad. You giving the streets something to talk about."

"I have my own life to live. I don't go any fucking where, Siris, so don't stand up here making me out to be this bad person. I never did anything to hurt my dad's reputation." I pointed my index finger in Osiris's face as tears leaped out of my eyes without warning. I was never the kind of person to cry about juvenile shit, but it was something about Osiris that made me break. His presence made me weak, which made me want to slap my damn self. I wasn't supposed to feel weak to no other man but Beatz. He was the one who truly understood me; the only one I could open up to without being judged.

The Hot Spot was only a few blocks from where I stayed. It was a place dedicated to the younger crowd, so we were able to have fun without drinking. When the youth club first opened up the street, I knew my pop wasn't going to let me go, so instead of asking, I attended against his will.

Trying to be perfect all the time made me want to run away from it all. I knew people watched my every move, and I was trying my best to stay out of the public's eye despite me sneaking out on the weekends to have a little fun.

"Lyric, I didn't mean to make you cry. Let me just take you home," Osiris said. I didn't need him or anybody else to feel sorry for me or give me a fucking pity. After he came at me wrong, the nigga was trying to make it right by offering to take me home.

"Whatever." I headed over to the passenger's door trying my best to dry my damn face.

"I'm sorry." Osiris was right on my heels, and opened the door for me. I knew he was doing all that shit because he didn't want to stay on my bad side.

I was quiet the whole ride until we reached my block. I was ready to talk then, and get some information out of his clown ass.

"What in the hell were you doing there anyway? Isn't the twenty-one and up club on the Southside?" I looked over at Osiris. I wanted to slap him upside his goofy ass head. Everybody was minding their business, finding something to get into, while he was stuck on what I had going on.

"I knew I would see you. I had this feeling you know." Osiris slowed the car down like he was about to let the windows down and air the streets out.

"Are you stalking me?" I raised my voice louder than I wished.

"Naw, I just have to make sure you're safe. It's my job to protect you,

Lyric, to make sure your family is straight while Don is on the road taking care of business." Osiris stopped the car a few houses down from mine. He turned off the headlights and looked at me with those eyes that would make any young bitch wet her panties. "Lyric, I know you're not digging me or nothing close, but I'm feeling you. I want the best for you. I want to be that nigga for you. Like, I'm not some fancy nigga. I won't buy you chocolate when you on your period and shit, but I'll show you the love you need. You're getting older, and the older you get the phonier these niggas are out here."

"Siris don't start this." I dropped my head. The moment he expressed his feelings made it clear to me that things would never go back to being the same. He wouldn't be just a nigga that's cool with my pop, a right hand to the Warriors, or any of that. Seeing him at the house would make it awkward, because although I had a hard ass feeling he was into me, his words made it all real.

"No, don't tell me to keep my feelings inside. Lyric, I'm the best man for you. Don knows this. We've even talked about this. Your dad approves of me. He knows I won't let anything happen to you." Osiris let it all out without trying to sugarcoat anything. I wish he spared me the truth.

"I don't know." I built up my nerves to look back up at Osiris. "I just don't know."

"Let me take you out to the city. Get to know me then you decide," Osiris replied.

"Okay." It was too fucking late to take my words back. I don't know what possessed me to agree on a date with Osiris. I don't know if it was the way he showed how much he cared about me, or maybe I was feeling him too and didn't realize it until that night. It was crazy how things unraveled. Then at the recognition of my words, my mind fell on Beatz. I was already riding for somebody, now I was caught up in the webs of Beatz and Osiris.

"Good, let's go tomorrow." Osiris reached over me to open door. The whole time he was doing so, it felt like I was going to drown in my thoughts; drown in the thought of laying on his sheets. It was funny how my heart betrayed me. How it betrayed Beatz, of all people.

* * *

"Lyric wake up, wake up." Lex snatched the cover off me.

"Why the fuck would you do that?" I sat upright on the bed. It was a Monday and Lex was supposed to be in school anyway.

After the night I had, the last thing I needed was for someone to wake me before the alarm went off.

"You know, Mall? The tall dark-skinned boy that be hanging with the Southside?" Lex narrowed her eyes across the room. She focused on the clock that kept ticking on the wall. "He was in a terrible car crash yesterday."

"He was killed on Mother's Day?" I bucked my eyes. "I can only imagine what his mother is going through."

"Yeah, and on top of that, people are saying he and his mother had an argument before he left the house that day. That's a shitty way to tell someone goodbye." Lex laid the news on me then she headed to the door to let herself out. "I heard there's a group from our territory that's going up the block to toss a few pair of his shoes on the power lines next to his momma's house then they are lighting candles."

"You want to go? I mean, I can call a few friends to tag along too." I finally unglued myself from the bed.

With Lex and I being daughters of the Eastside Warriors' honcho, it was our duty to show up to pay respect, no matter how it tugged with our emotions. Me above my younger sisters, I had to be involved with the things that were going on in the streets. My pop told me long ago that it was my duty to make sure the hood felt like I was for the hood and not just living off his name alone.

However, his name was what kept us protected. It made the neighborhood loyal to us. If it wasn't for the weight my pop's name held out there, without a doubt, I would've been another target for the niggas in the hood that pimped out young girls from the Eastside all the way to the Southside. But, they knew not to cross that line with Don's girls.

"Yeah, that's cool." Lex walked out of the room.

Once Lex was out of the room, I walked over to the mirror. I wasn't expecting to face something like that. I wasn't even close to the boy who died, but people on the block were like family; our family. Pop made it very clear when I was barely able to understand street life completely, that our family was bigger than blood ties. We had extended family out of loyalty. Above all, the Warriors were our family, and if I wasn't mistaking, Mall was a new member of the Warriors gang, so we had lost a family member.

Heading over to my closet to pick out an appropriate outfit to wear to the Shoe Toss, I mumbled, "Lord." The thought of death alone made my soul uneasy. I felt sorry for his mother. She lost her only son. To be honest, I was sorry his life was cut short.

When I finished getting dressed for the Shoe Toss, I headed into the living room to wait on Lex, who was in the kitchen eating a late breakfast. When things like this happens, food is the last thing on my mind while Lex is the complete opposite.

"I think it's good of the two of you to go over there to the Shoe Toss." Pop strolled into the living room in the middle of lighting a cigarette. There was never a day that went by without him being spotted with a cigarette in his hand; no matter how many times momma cussed his ass out for doing so.

"Well, you've always taught us to do the right thing and that's what I'm trying to do," I replied.

"You know, I always thought I'd have boys and they'd grow up to carry all of this out for me, but God didn't see my life that way. He gave me three girls." Pop took a steady puff of the cigarette then let the smoke out through his nostrils. "He gave me girls because he knew they would be strong."

"It don't seem like I'm doing too much of nothing, though. You don't let me in on what it is you're doing out there. All I know is that my pop is this respected man around here that's the honcho of the Eastside Warriors. Trust, I have my wild guesses of what you do, I just don't want to believe that you're like all those other crews that take innocent lives," I said in one breath.

"You will know when the time is right," Pop replied.

"And when will the time be right? You want me to be a part of this, to keep your legacy going and all that by doing right by the neighborhood?" I rose from the couch. My attitude sometimes arrived out of nowhere. Whenever it did show up, it was always too late for me to tame it.

"Since when do you have the balls to question me? Now, we were on good terms. Let's keep it that way." Pop looked at me like I'd lost my mind. No matter how old I was or would be, it was never my place to disrespect my pop.

"Sorry." I backed down.

"You ready?" Lex walked into the living like she'd been given a dose of energy. She was always high on her heels and ready to get the day started. Between Lex and me, Pop mentioned one time that he wasn't sure who deserved to be the reigning leader of his empire when he was ready to step down. But, he knew that it was only fair to give me the responsibility since I was the oldest. Although I would never grow the balls to tell him, I didn't want to rule anything. All I wanted to do was move out of state to the West Coast with Beatz and chase my dreams as a music artist.

"Yeah, let's go." I walked ahead of Lex, trying my best to get out of sight and out of fucking mind. My pop didn't care how old we got, he would still jack us up real quick. Not no beating with no belt either, he laid hands on us like we were niggas. It was a lesson he claimed to be teaching us. He wanted to teach us strength while instilling his fear; fear to never cross him or he would cross us.

"When the streetlight comes on." He made sure he reminded us that no matter how good of a job we were doing out there, we still had his rules to follow.

"We know," I blurted out.

# OSIRIS

While the streets were occupied with the death of one of our own, I was busy ensuring I was ahead of the game and kept Don's empire on top. Three years ago, Don was named the biggest drug dealer in the south and we were set on keeping it that way.

"This better be good. I was just handling business at home when you called, so what's up?" Don took a seat opposite me.

Whenever I invited Don over, I made sure to have some cigarettes on deck along with a nice personal bottle of Remi Martin. I was always trying to do right by Don because if it wasn't for Don, I would've been serving my first decade in the state penitentiary for first-degree murder and armed robbery. But, Don made sure he went out of his way to help a young man who made a terrible mistake.

"You think Mall's death was really a legit accident?" Since hearing the news about Mall losing his life in a car crash, my mind has been in overload. It is crazy to me that he died one month after officially being initiated into the Eastside Warriors clan.

"They were drinking and doing whatever else. I don't have any reason to suspect it was a hit on our gang," Don replied.

"Alright then, I'll let it go. But on another note, how much do you know about Young Dro's crew out in Atlanta?" I asked.

Don focused on pouring him a glass of Remy Martin while lighting a cigarette in the process. He finally turned his attention back to me after a while. "Not a damn thing. Why?"

"Well, he contacted me earlier this morning. He wants to do business with us; with you." I lit a blunt while waiting to hear what Don had to say about the situation. Don was the boss and it was his call whether we went into business with another crew.

"Naw, you know I don't do business with people I'm not familiar with. I'm not hungry. My members are eating. We're in no need to make the company bigger." Don took a sip of whiskey. His eyes stayed on me the entire time. He leaned forward on the seat. "Do you know how niggas get busted?"

"How?" I asked.

"They never let well enough be. They're always hungry for more; more money, more power, and more power. I'm comfortable here in the position that I'm in. My house is paid off, cars are paid off, bills are never late and my muthafuckin' hood loves me." Don slammed the glass onto the glass end table. He stood. "Next time just tell me what it's about over the phone."

"Yes sir." I followed Don's lead and saw him out of the house. "Can I ask you something?"

"Go ahead." Don stopped in his tracks.

"I know this has nothing to do with business or anything." I was searching for the right words so that I wouldn't get on Don's bad side.

"Can you hurry up? I still owe Brier a date since I missed celebrating with her on Mother's Day." Don wasn't the kind of person to endure people taking their precious time to ask him something. He was a busy man and he didn't have time to waste. I understood that, so I never tried to waste his time with any just bullshit.

"Do you think Lyric will grow to see past all of this? I mean, once she finds out what I do, all the things that I've done?" I wanted to punch my damn self in the face for sounding like a punk ass nigga.

"Siris, I don't feel like discussing my daughter right now. Just make sure you keep her safe tonight. Just because you're my right hand doesn't mean you're exempt from getting hands laid on you if something happens to her." Don nudged me on the shoulder then he dipped.

* * *

"You're really serious about being with her huh?" Jab took a hit of the blunt then passed it back to me.

"Yeah, she's different than all the hoes out here bruh. She wasn't raised like the bitches you see flocking to niggas that have a lil' bankroll. She knows what it means and feels to have something. Not just anybody is going to excite a girl like that." Out of all the people I was cool with, I didn't trust anyone with my personal business but Jab. He never mind telling me what he thought was best while listening to my reason for how he was wrong.

"I feel all of that, but what happens if shit doesn't work out between the two of you? Or if you mess up? Then Don is going to be on yo' ass and looking at you strange. What happened to you never mixing your business with personal?" Jab said.

"I told you before; I'm not going to fuck up. And I'm not mixing business with personal." I took a drag of the blunt. Jab's words hit a certain way. If Don really did step down in the empire and allow Lyric to be the boss, I was going to be going against my number one rule. *Never mix business with pleasure.*

"Aside from all that you have goin' on, when are you going to get out? You've been rocking with Don in the life of crime since you were like seventeen. That's ten whole years, bruh. Ten. That's a long time to give someone your life because they saved yours." Jab walked around the room a bit. He told me he's been doing a lot of thinking lately about where he wanted to go and the things he wanted to do with his life. And, with him changing up, it meant he was going to be leaving behind a few people until he got his life together; including me.

"Jab, c'mon man, you already know how it goes. I can't leave now. I know too much about his business. If I ever try to run off on Don, he'll have me offed. There's no way out." I scratched the back of my head. I could never stress enough how Don saved me. I would go the rest of my life just to pay it all back.

"Well, I just want to let you know that I was serious when I told you I'm getting out of here. Like, I have dreams bigger than this town. I want to produce movies for a living, and I can't do that here because there are no opportunities." Jab hit his hands together. "This town will pull you down and keep you here if you allow it. I don't want to perish where I was born."

"I hear you." That day Jab made me think long and hard about the path I was on. Still, the bitterness of never being able to leave Don's crew brought me back to the vow I made. I was in it for life. "I'm 'bout to roll out though."

"Alright bruh," Jab said.

I made it back to the house right before Mom Duke pulled into the driveway. I spoke to her before she went to her appointment. I offered to take her, but she turned me down without any explanation. I just assumed she needed her space, so I let her be.

When she made it inside, she didn't even let me know. All I heard was the front door close. I walked out of my room into the kitchen. She was sitting at the table with her head down. I took a seat in front of her with my heart in a strain. I hated the feeling of overthinking situations.

"They believe its cancer. I won't know for sure until all the tests come back." Mom Duke let out through what seemed like a cry and a laugh.

"Cancer? What kind of cancer?" My heart dropped to the bottom of my stomach. She had been sick on and off for years. She kept telling me she was alright and not to worry about her. She was fine.

"Stage four Breast Cancer." Mom Duke viewed me with a smile on her face. I couldn't understand what she found lighthearted about her possibly having cancer. All I thought about was having to plan a funeral, and being left alone without her guidance.

"Ma this ain't nothing light. We have to take this serious and do whatever we can to get this under control," I said.

"Baby calm down. Can you do that for me?" She rested her hands on the table. I don't know what I saw in her eyes at the table. I'm not sure if it was her giving in to the sickness or her knowing she was going to overcome it.

"I just don't know what to do. Tell me how can I help you? There has to be something that I can do." I had always been able to keep my emotions hidden. I wanted to be strong for everyone, regardless of the hardships I faced. But, seeing how down Mom Duke was, knowing she was sick and there was nothing I could do about it, made me shed tears.

"Siris, if it's really stage four cancer, there's nothing anyone can do. No matter what kind of doctors I try to find, their answers are all going to be the same. I waited too long. I allowed this sickness to get the better of me. Ain't nobody did this to me but myself. If I would've gone to the doctor all those years back, I wouldn't be going through this today." Mom Duke took a deep breath like having a conversation zapped all her energy. "I just need my children to be strong. If I don't pull through, I need y'all to hold it together. Lean on each other when times are hard and love each other even when it feels impossible. That's all I want. There's only the three of you left now. Love each other."

"Ma, I hear you and all, but you're going to make it. You have to make it. I know I walk 'round here like I'm the strongest man alive, but I'm nothing without you." I stood from the chair and took quick strides over to Mom Duke. She was the center of my world. She was the glue that kept everything together. "It's not fair. None of this is fair. Why can't God go mess with someone else?"

I took lives all the time and offed niggas without thinking about it on account of Don. It was easy for me. I hadn't dealt with the death of a loved one since I lost my older brother at the hand of some hating ass niggas. Not sure if I ever dealt with it, though. All I did was find the niggas responsible and caused their families pain too. I got even.

Mom Duke wrapped her arms around me as best as she could. "Because God takes each of us through different things. It's not our job to question Him."

"It doesn't make it right what He's allowing you to go through." I shook my head as the tears never shied away from making a mess of my face. I couldn't hide my pain. It was my Mom Duke sitting there who was given the bitter end of life. I never saw her do anything bad or wronged anybody. All she ever tried to do was make peace and have fun. When my brother was murdered, she refused to point fingers at anybody. She told me time and time again to leave it to God to judge.

She later released me and went inside her room to be alone. To see someone you love suffer was a different kind of heartache. It was like I was suffering with her.

I barged out the door with a heavy heart. Nothing looked the same. The neighborhood felt strange. The aroma of the air smelled toxic. It pained me to know that long after she was gone the world was going to continue. Her sweet personality would only be a memory. People who knew her was only going speak of her in the past tense, reminiscing on the times they shared, and the laughs she brought.

"Ayyye, what's good savage? Looks like you're having a rough day," Hastine shouted from across the street. With niggas like him watching my every move, I had to put the emotions aside. All it took was one nigga to know I was slipping to off me. I couldn't have that.

"Ain't nothing new bruh. I'm good over here," I shouted back. It was shameful for a thug to cry. Thank God it wasn't part of the code to not shed tears, because then I would've been a disloyal, weak ass nigga.

## LYRIC

When me and my crew of four arrived at the Shoe Toss, we had to nearly fight our way through the crowd. Although some cliques stayed to themselves, most of them came together for the cause.

"Did you really have to invite both of them?" Lex sighed. Whenever she tagged along with me, Cassie and Monique weren't too far behind. It seemed like Lex was always trying to fight for my attention whenever my friends were around. She didn't have to though, because there wasn't any female who could take the place of my sister.

"Girl be quiet." I focused on getting through the thick crowd.

"Yeah." Lex backed down. It wasn't the proper place to be all up my face about juvenile problems, so it was better for Lex to throw the whole little dispute in the trash.

The whole time I was there, I fought my hardest to stay in control of my emotions. Being there made it all real. The hood lost another soul, that wasn't due to any kind of gang violence, and it was tragic that nobody saw it coming.

Then to top it all off, I kept thinking about when my pop was going to give me his responsibility without giving me a say in the decision. I knew having his title, I'd be front and center for more tragedies. People were going to be coming to me expecting to receive the same treatment my pop gave them.

"Damn," Cassie said while looking straight ahead at Osiris tossing a pair of shoes on the line. She was drooling over him like he was the finest nigga she ever saw, and he probably was. Osiris wasn't an average nigga from the hood; he was fine even on his worse days. I would always be last to admit it to his face.

"What?" I already knew who Cassie was drooling over, and somebody drooling over Osiris never made me feel uneasy. I couldn't deny the gut of annoyance that washed over me from the words that came out of Cassie's mouth.

"Isn't that the man who be over there with Mr. Don?" Cassie waved over at Osiris.

"Yeah, and?" I rolled my eyes at the thought of Cassie trying to get with Osiris.

"I need that in my life Sis. Hook me up." Cassie made sure Osiris saw the way she was eyeballing him. Unlike most girls her age, she wasn't looking for some young nigga on the streets who were jumping from girl to girl. She's trying to score her a mature man that was going to keep food in her mouth while she chased her dreams.

"I would, but he's already trying to holla at me." I waved at Osiris too.

"Let me know if you turn him down or not, because bitch believe me, I will turn him on and have him hooked for life." Cassie shifted all her weight to one leg as she wrapped her hair around her finger.

I blocked Cassie completely out while in disbelief. I mentioned Osiris trying to get with me to make her back off him. I steered clear of all my pop's minions, still none of them were bold enough to try to be with me like Osiris. Aside from working with my pop, I heard he had an almost murder charge years ago. He was heading down the road, but like the nobleman my pop was, he managed to get Osiris out of the system.

"Hellooooo," Monique yelled in my face like she lost her fucking mind. The bitch knew damn well it irritated my soul when someone pulled something like that. "Did you hear me?"

"Bitch what?" Why the fuck are you all in my face like that?" I gently pushed Monique back before I bucked on her. She out of everybody knew not to be all up in my face. I whooped a bitch down bad last time that happened.

"Do you want to sing out here? There's already too many shoes on that power line, so I thought it'll be best if we do a little performance," Monique suggested.

"You already know I don't sing. That's your thing," I replied.

"Cassie and I will sing, and you do what you do best." Monique was already making her way in the center of the crowd to get everyone's attention. Unlike Cassie and me, Monique longed for attention. She was always singing in front of people for praise or just dressing down to the T to make boys drool over the little ass she had. With all the shit she did to make niggas turn their head, they still flocked to me when we were in the same space. I made niggas stop and stare whenever I entered a room, with my nice coke bottle shape to match my pretty face. Wasn't no bitch going to steal my shine, and I didn't even try to save it.

"Lead the way then." I shrugged my shoulders at Lex who was standing behind me with her arms up. We were supposed to be there for one reason only. Knowing Lex, I knew she liked keeping a low profile at places. She had a group of friends who showed her enough attention. The center of attention wasn't ever her style, and she knew I was the same way but always got swindled in by my peers. I sometimes had to let the bitches know I wasn't scared of being in the spotlight whenever it presented itself.

"Me and my girls would like to sing a song if that's okay with everyone." Monique stood in the middle; me and Cassie occupied her sides. The crowd cheered for us and Monique broke down in a song that I never heard her sing. The song was flowing so well, there was no doubt in my mind that Monique already knew what she was going to sing to shine. Like there were a handful of songs we rehearsed together, so it would've been easy to choose from any of them.

"We grew up on the same block. He speaks, I speak when he pass by. Not a stranger when you look a man in the eye. Life too short to let it pass by. You dodge four bullets and escape out, but when the stopwatch stops ticking you ran your time out." I collaborated on the song whenever Monique gave me the cue to rap something. Freestyling wasn't my strong suit; I never backed down from any challenge though.

Once we finished with the pop-up performance, I saw Osiris cutting through the crowd walking towards me. I owed him a date, which made my heart shrink a little. I never went out with any dude besides Beatz, but our situation was different. He was my friend, one of my best male friends to date, and it was easy being next to him. I felt like one of the homies whenever we hung out. One of the homies whenever we weren't naked underneath each other.

"You haven't forgotten about me, huh?" Osiris said once he was facing me. The whole time he was talking to me, Cassie was behind him, still drooling over him like she didn't have knowledge of me saying he was basically off limits.

"Shit, after today I'm not even sure if I want to do anything. I feel really bad for his mom," I said. I never confided in anyone and there I was willing to tell him exactly how I was feeling. "I just hate when people die. It brings all this anxiety out of me."

"I feel you, but you know time doesn't slow down for anyone, and stressing yourself about things that's beyond your control will only make you lose time that you won't be able to get back. So, with all of that being said, let me take you out to get your mind right." Osiris placed his hand on my shoulder like I already belonged to him. And as crazy as it was to admit, I no longer saw anything wrong with being his woman.

"My pop won't let me go on a date. I guess we both forgot about how protective he is of me," I replied with an apologetic smile.

"I already told him that I'm taking you out after the Shoe Toss and that I'll make sure Lex gets home safe. I'm always two steps ahead," Osiris said.

"You lying. I know you think you have my pop wrapped around your finger, but when it comes to me, it's a completely different game." Using my pop as an excuse got me out of a lot of things, but I couldn't hide behind his overprotectiveness with Osiris. He was like the man with a masterplan.

"I don't have no reason to lie. You can phone him right now. I would never lie on Don's name. He trusts me as his right hand and to handle all his business affairs, so he knows how I'm coming. Lying is something I don't do. That's the fuckin code." Osiris said those words with his eyes never leaving mine.

"Damn, calm down. You don't have to get all tight on me." I raised my hands in defense. I witnessed how Osiris could get when someone accused him. He was big on making sure his name was protected on the streets. He didn't do rumors and sure as hell never took pity on someone who tried their best to tarnish his name. I overheard how fed up he was one day when he came to pay my pop a visit, it seemed like it took forever to calm him down.

"I'm not being tight on you. I'm just letting you know how I get down," Osiris said.

"Yeah, aight." I let it slide. Osiris was the first man that made me behave that way. It was like I wanted to listen to him, while the other part of me wanted to challenge him in every way.

\* \* \*

"Loosen up. I'm not going to bite you unless you like a nigga biting you and shit." Osiris took a drag of his blunt.

"You be knocking niggas off the map for my pop too?" I pointed to the pistol that rested on the dashboard. Osiris was always a question to me. The business between him and my pop left me in question more than once. It was just that Osiris came off a bit ruthless. There was no telling what he did to uphold the gang, or who he murdered to be in Pop's good grace.

"You serious about being a rapper?" Osiris changed subjects to get himself out of the limelight. He wasn't smooth like he thought he was, though. I peeped game.

"Real smooth." I folded my arms. We were having a good time being together that night, so instead of trying to dig the truth out of him, I allowed him to touch basis on a deeper level that was intriguing for us both. "But yeah, I'm very serious about it. I rock the mic like no other. I know people hear it all the time about bitches trying to be the queen of rap. I know I can be the queen. I'm dope as fuck and don't know any female that has a flow like me."

"Confidence. I can dig that." Osiris took a long steady drag of the blunt, and blew the smoke out through his nose like he did it on the regular.

"What do you do outside of being loyal to my pop?" I was still kind of digging around to see what kind of life Osiris lived. "You're always standoffish and secretive. You pretty much know all there is to know about me and my family, so tell me something I don't know about you."

"Being loyal to your dad and being his right hand is something that takes a big part of my life. I know you tired of me saying it, but working for him is my life, Lyric. There's no way out of it. I vowed to do business with and for him until my dying day." Osiris laid it out there for me.

In the middle of Osiris spilling his truth, his phone started going off. "Shit, let me take this call real quick."

While Osiris was on the phone, I made it my business to send Beatz a text message about studio time. He was willing to help me with the career that felt farfetched. If nobody believed in my dream, Beatz believed, and would stand up to anybody on my behalf. He was the kind of friend every girl wanted without the strings attached. We could talk for hours at a time and not get bored. We had the kind of connection that sparked a fire. A connection so strong we couldn't help but to fall for each other and get caught up in our own strings.

Osiris started the engine to the car, pulled out of the dimmed parking space, and headed onto the main road. After he received the phone, it put him in a shitty mood.

"I know I had this whole date thing planned, but something is going on at the warehouse. They said somebody set it on fire." Osiris's voice was filled with bottled up uneasiness. He mentioned the *warehouse* like it was something familiar to me, but I didn't have a single clue of what the fuck he was talking about.

"The warehouse?" I questioned.

"Don's business establishment was hit like fifteen minutes ago. They thinking it's some enemies trying to off him; start some drama out there; something." Osiris focused on the road ahead

"What enemies Siris? What's going on?" I looked over at Osiris waiting for him to further explain what the hell was going on. Without knowing much about it, I knew it was serious, and the nerves that formed in my belly made me feel like I had to vomit.

"Just be quiet for a minute I'm trying to think." Osiris checked the rearview mirror a few times before he picked up his phone again. "I need you to be heading his way, boss. Trever just told me that warehouse two is on fire and I'm already in route."

"Alright, I'll be there in a few. I have to make a stop before I head that way," I heard my pop's voice blast from the speakerphone. "Is Lyric still with you?"

"Okay, I'll be keeping you updated until you make it and yeah, she's still with me. You know I won't let anything happen to her." Osiris got a glimpse of me before turning his attention back on the road ahead.

"Don't tell her what's really going on right now. I would like to explain all of this myself. And if it's really bad, I'll have to get the family together as a whole." Right after my pop said those words, Osiris quickly took the phone off of speaker.

No matter what threat my pop's crew was facing, he was going to protect his family at all cost, even if it meant bringing harm to someone else's family. Being a protector and provider was his sole purpose as husband and father, and he wasn't going to go to his grave without living out his duties. He made sure he let us know that as long as he was alive there was nothing to worry about. He wouldn't let any harm come near us.

"Yes, I gotcha boss. Be careful out there." Osiris ended the phone call.

Before I could summon up any questions, Osiris had already made it to the parking lot of the warehouse and hopped out the car. Being loyal to my pop meant he had to be ten toes down and willing to take the bullet whenever shit went left. It made me wonder why the hell he was trying to get my time when he could've died out there trying to live up to the code of the gang.

# LEX

With a pop like mine, any girl would feel protected; like nobody in the world could mess with her. I never felt that way though, I was too busy dealing with the anxiety that made me a victim since as early as I could remember. Most people in the hood never liked owning up to their mental being damaged, however, I was open to the people I was able to be open with. It didn't matter what kind of upbringing a person had being raised in the hood, the environment had a way of beating anybody to their knees.

"That's why I don't smoke with your ass now. You be getting deep in your thoughts." Michael snatched the blunt out my hand quicker than I was able to react to his sudden swiping.

"Man, really? You gon' do me like that? You know I only get to kick it once in a blue moon." My words came out slower to me than I believe to Michael. I don't know what he put in that blunt, but I was done.

"So, how you managed to sneak out this time?" Michael took a whiff from the blunt. His eyes rolled to the back like he snorted an entire line of coke. Being with Michael made me forget that we weren't even legal yet since we did the most adult things when we were together.

Aside from the other two friends I had, he really understood me. He was never the type of person to judge me or make me feel like I couldn't feel down because of who my pop was out there on the streets.

"There was an emergency and he had to dip, so I took a run out the back door during the commotion. Although my momma checks our rooms sometimes, she never takes it hard on me or snitches when she notices I'm not there. It's our lil' thing." I grabbed the blunt back from Michael, and took a steady drag, allowing the smoke to settle, before blowing it out. Back when I was an amateur at getting high, Michael used to charge it to me, and I swear it fucked me up every time. As time progressed, we only charged it to each other for the fun of it. Away from home, I was a completely different person. At home, I was the quiet teenager who never asked for a damn thing; always kept my mouth shut. However, with my friends, I was the person that was trying to find myself by joking around and being reckless whenever I received the right opportunity.

"And you ain't worried 'bout what's going on? You know Mr. Don has a lot of enemies out there. Hell, I don't see how a man like him even sleeps at night knowing that very fact." Michael reached for the blunt again to take his hit, but all I had to pass back was a butt. We'd been blazing for what felt like hours. Sometimes we smoked so much it made me vomit. That was a dead giveaway that I needed to slow down.

"I do worry enough on a daily, so there's no need in using my last bit of energy on something that's beyond me," I said.

"I dig that. How do you feel 'bout what happened to Mall? Like, I know you, your sister and 'em went to the Shoe Toss." Michael hung around everybody, so he pretty much knew about everything that happened in town without having to be in an exact location.

"How does a person feel 'bout any death? It's tragic. It woke me up though. Life isn't promised to anybody, and that's real." I laid back on Michael's bed. Death was something I thought about more than anybody I knew to date. A fear would overtake me sometimes and worried me until my palms turned pale and caused my heart to flutter. I wasn't clinically diagnosed with any mental unstableness, but anybody walking a day in my shoes knew something was wrong.

"Shit, shit." Michael grabbed the air freshener can from the nightstand. He sprayed around the room like he'd lost his mind. Smoking weed wasn't sin on the block, but to Michael's pop, it was. Mr. Griffin was a hardcore Muslim who practiced the faith with every intention of going to heaven.

"I thought you said he was out of town?" I removed myself from the bed as quick as my stoned body would allow. With Mr. Griffin being extra serious about his beliefs, Michael wasn't permitted to have girls over, but that didn't stop him from sneaking me in or sleeping around when he got the chance.

"He was supposed to be." Michael raised his bedroom window up to air out the room and to let me slip out so neither of us would be in trouble. Mr. Griffin didn't mind getting other parents involved. He believed discipline started at home. But if he only knew what kind of discipline happened at our house, he would've felt sorry and kept his mouth closed. The last time I did something rebellious and my pop found out, he fist fought me like a nigga. And in his house, we weren't allowed to fight back; we had to bow to him and accept the beatings with open arms.

"Text me when you make it home." Michael gave me a boost out the window and I fell right out. I was too fucked up to be trying to sneak out his window after blazing like that.

"Okay," I murmured through the pain of being scraped by the rough windowpane.

\* \* \*

"What the fuck are you doing on this side of the hood bitch? You know your kind isn't welcomed here." Favo and a group of other men had somebody cornered. I couldn't see who it was, not that it was my business anyway. Pop always said that if it doesn't concern me, then don't go looking for trouble on somebody's account. Living by that saying kept a lot of people in the hood alive. However, it was hard for me to stand by and let somebody get beat down to their death. Our hood was supposed to be about unity; peace. We were supposed to be one big ass family. We'd just lost one of our own in a car crash, now they were working on bringing heartache to another family's doors.

Favo was older than I was by five years. He was twenty-one and I was at the tender age of sixteen with a whole lot of heart. Every man, woman, and child respected my pops and his crew. So, me intervening with what they had going on wasn't going to get me murdered in cold blood. They knew what was up; especially Favo. Just several months ago, Pop's right hand, Osiris, beat him to his knees for doing reckless shit on the block. Favo lost both front teeth at the cost of his actions.

"Is that what we're all about now? Terrorizing people?" I blurted those words without thinking clearly. All I really knew was that whatever they were planning to do wasn't going to happen on my watch.

"Lil' bitch you best gon' on your way before you get this big, gangsta dick too," the man that stood beside Favo shouted. There was no doubt he was in the dark on who the fuck he was speaking to. His face was new to me, and that rarely happened. Maybe he was just visiting or something because there wasn't a face I didn't know that stayed on the Eastside.

"I would love to see you try it nigga." I pulled out my purple .22 Glock that Michael bought for my past birthday. He kept telling me I needed a gun for my protection when I wasn't under my pop's wings because with the temper I possessed, it would no doubt land me in some bad company. That night his words manifested. "Now leave her alone before I blow your fuckin' head off. You must not know which set I rep and who the fuck my pop is."

"Bitch, fuck your set; you think I give a fuck? I do this shit for fun. Hop city-to-city fuckin' bitches with mouths like you. If you gon' shot then you better fuckin' shoot because if not I'm gon' lay some pipe to ya." He talked like a drunk man, and his body was moving all kind of ways like he was out of it.

"Naw, back off man. You don't want those problems." Favo pulled the man back out of recognition of who I was. Everybody in town knew better than to fuck with Don's family. Some tried it a few times in the past; they never lived to see another week either. My pop handled things his own way but it got handled.

"Man, naw fuck it. I want all those problems. Pop that lil' bitch's pussy and have her bleeding for days." The man talked back to me like he was tough. See, most niggas underestimated me. I was a lil' crazy; screwed up in the brain. I had heart, never walked around trying to be all girly-girl. I was a hood nigga at heart.

"Make this bleed." I pulled the trigger, shooting a cap right through his testicles. I never capped. If I said I was going to do something, I went through with it without a frown. It's what I was all about. The life I led.

"Fuck, bruh. I told you. I told you." Favo hit the ground running along with two other men, leaving the man that I popped to fall on the wet lawn alone. He cried with the loudest cry I ever heard escape from someone.

"Thank you." The woman's face was beaten up to the pink meat. If she wasn't so bruised, I probably would've been able to recognize her.

"Just get out of here." I put my Glock away and finally headed home as I intended before being sidetracked.

Michael stayed down on Circle Drive, which was literally right up the street from where I lived. Between walking and a slight jog, I was home quicker than I could count to one hundred.

When I made it inside it was quiet. So quiet that I was able to hear my thoughts bounce from wall to wall. Lyric went out with Osiris earlier in the day, so the first thing I did was check to see if she made it in, and to my surprise, the room was still empty. Osiris had to be one of Pop's most loyal Warriors to allow Lyric to be out past curfew. And Lyric had to be really feeling Osiris to be out with him knowing she started talking to Beatz on a deeper level. Nobody else knew but the three of us. It was still disheartening to know that she was doing Beatz in after they'd been friends for years and were now in a *situationship,* as she called it many times.

Away from all of the drama that didn't belong to me, I broke down in the middle of the bedroom floor with an empty feeling that wouldn't subside. While my pop was busy ruling the streets and caring for the community, he was losing his daughter with each passing day. It was like each morning was harder and harder. The pain was growing like wildfire and if I didn't receive the proper help, it was going to consume me altogether.

*Why won't this emptiness go away?* I thought with tears running down my cheeks. One minute I felt alive and the next hopeless. I tried telling myself I had every reason to be happy, but it all felt like one big lie. Because what did I really have to live for?

# BEATZ

When I was heading over to Lyric, she was busy talking to Osiris, the infamous right hand of the Eastside Warriors. When he called her name as we were leaving the Hot Spot, I saw how she reacted in recognition of his presence, but I let it go because I knew how the gang went. She didn't want to upset Don if Osiris rat on her about being out with me after-hours. When I saw her chopping it up with him at the Shoe Toss, her body language told it all; she was feeling him. He was moving in on the girl that I was deeply sprung over. I was in love with Lyric. I had been loving her since we were children, although the love was different then. Now she was all up in another nigga's face like we hadn't set our relationship in stone, or like we hadn't just boned.

"I knew you would show up." T-Max met me at the gate of the 211 Vipers HQ. He had his AR-15 prepared to off any man that tried to off him first. As he opened the gates, my stomach tied in knots. I had no reason being there besides being angry with Lyric. I figured since she was a new fan of thugged out niggas, I would be just that for her. Then on top of that, music wasn't really pulling in no money and I was tired of seeing my mom struggle to pay the bills while all I was giving her was a pipe dream.

"How so?" I walked into the territory with my heart slowly coming to a calm. I felt at home like 211s were welcoming me back home after being gone forever. I was new to it though; never stepped foot beyond those gates. My conscious was getting the better of me too. I was about to become a true enemy of the Eastside Warriors. Don was going to have a target on my back for life, until I was six feet under.

"Because a man always finds his way home." T-Max closed the gates behind me in urgency. He peeped around the facility to see if I brought any company. When he noted there was nobody out there, he led me inside of the building with his AR-15 still close to his side.

The inside of the building looked nothing like the outside. The outside looked abandoned; like some old ass warehouse, but the inside was luxurious. It outshined any office building I ever entered. I never owned expensive things; I just knew them when I laid eyes on them.

"Who the fuck let you up in here? Looking like a knockout off version of Drake." A man walked into the lobby with a Classic 9mm resting in his waistband.

"This is Cappo's nephew. His brother's son." T-Max introduced. He failed to tell the tall, beefy dude my name. With a name like *Beatz*, I knew he wasn't going to take me seriously.

"Cappo's uptight nephew you mean. The one who thinks he's too good to be part of the 211s because he's sprung like a lil' bitch over an Eastside hoe." The man's voice was deep and filled with authority. He looked like he was hitting his fifties hard. It didn't stop him from appearing every bit of intimidating.

"Well, circumstances have changed, and he's stepping up to lead the gang." T-Max spoke with all the confidence a man could possess for another. He believed I was able to be a great honcho like my uncle and cousin. I just prayed I was able to prove him right and not make him look like a fool out there on the streets. Unlike the people I was going to be leading, I never shot a gun. I knew the names of guns from playing all the Call of Duties. That was it though.

"Lead the gang? Who gave you the authority to make a decision like that? I don't give a flame fuck about Cappo Alejo's blood flowing through his veins. That was twenty years ago; thirteen years since the last Alejo honcho died. We been surviving since, so what makes you think we need another one of them to lead us?" The man gave his strong disapproval of me trying to step up in the shoes of honcho.

"Phons, last I checked, I've always been next in rank. You're two ranks underneath me, so don't go around trying to challenge my authority. We don't do that 'round here. You know better." T-Max strolled past Phons with me closely following his lead. With me being crowned as the honcho, there was no doubt that T-Max was going to teach me the ropes.

"Don't even worry 'bout him. He'll fall in line," T-Max said as he walked down the dimmed hallway. We passed by a few doors before we reached the last. He opened the door to the last room, and I followed him inside. Before we were in the office good, the smell of Kush filled my nostrils mixed with another strong scent.

"Welcome to the office." T-Max walked over to the black chest. Then he made his way back over to me, holding two fat blunts in his hands. Out my almost nineteen years of being alive, I never touched any kind of drugs. Nothing. I was what people considered as a *square*.

"Damn. This a dope ass space here." I took a stroll around the huge office space before taking a seat at the desk. I accepted the blunt like I blazed on the regular. I fired it up like a cigarette and took a big ass puff. That was the first mistake of the day. The smoke set my nostrils on fire, and it choked me up big time. It took me a good three minutes to get in control of the coughs. "Goddamn."

Through chuckles, T-Max spoke. "You really is a fuckin square; or was. I have to get you tougher than this weak shit. Don't ever just take a big drag like that on the first few hits. It makes you look like an amateur. Be patient with the blunt."

"Hmuh, word." I held in the tenth cough like my life depended on it.

"You know you can't expect people to respect you without being properly initiated in the 211s." T-Max smoked the Kush at a steady pace, blowing it out of his nostril effortlessly. He poured a glass of rum and slid it across the table to me. Now I drunk a few times before, not any naked whiskey though; always mixed mine. I felt niggas were retarded for downing naked whiskey.

"And how do I get properly initiated?" I accepted the brown poison. I downed the liquor and it instantly set my chest on fire. It burned all the way down. Once it reached my stomach, it felt like lava was bubbling around.

"You have to make a hit on a rival team. Chose which nigga you want to give the smoke to," T-Max replied. Osiris was at the top of my list since he made his move on Lyric. I never understood what my Old Head was saying when he told me; *a woman can turn a man mad.* That was right before he went rogue on a nigga for sleeping with my momma behind his back. I always wondered if he regret it now that he was still facing twenty years after serving ten.

"Let me hit Don where it hurts," I said. Suggesting a hit on Don was savage of me. I didn't know anybody boss enough to make a hit on the most feared man in the state.

"Oh, you trying to come like that huh? I thought you were macking on Lyric. What's she going to say if she finds out you initiated a hit on her dad?" T-Max smoked the blunt down to the butt while mine burned away without me taking another drag.

"This doesn't have nothing to do with Lyric. This ain't even personal,"

I said. Sitting there in front of T-Max, I was wishing there was somehow I could redo the entire day. What I was about to do was going to be a war of no return. Don was at the top of the list of 211 Vipers anyway, so if I could make a hit on him successfully, they were going to praise me.

"Oh, everything is personal and you're about to learn that." T-Max stood from the chair with a devilish chuckle.

* * *

T-Max and I were scoping out the place all evening. The whole time my stomach burned from the liquor I consumed earlier and the fact that my relationship with Lyric wasn't ever going to be the same.

"Alright, alright, we have a man on the inside. He has to destroy the security system before we make a move." T-Max spoke with his eyes glued to an expensive pair of binoculars.

"They have cameras?" I swallowed down what felt like shards of glass. If they failed to do the cameras correctly, Don was going to have my face and make me a target until he banished me.

"No shit. You think somebody like Don wouldn't have cameras in his spot. That's why we have somebody taking care of it now." T-Max said those words like he was tired of me talking, so I refused to speak until the whole hit was behind us.

About fifteen minutes into us scoping the warehouse out, it was time to move in while they were busy loading the truck out for shipment. If I had the names correct, the man that oversaw the warehouse that night for Don was Trever. I never saw him around, a few of the other faces I knew though.

"You take upstairs and I got down. Make it quick. Drench it then ignite it. You go ghost afterward. Wait in the getaway car for me." T-Max pointed two fingers forward. I followed his orders to the T. It was my idea to make the hit; however, T-Max was the one to hash the plan. If we stayed on track, the plan was going to be a success.

It took me about a minute to make it all the way upstairs on the second floor and when I was finally up there, I waited behind the main wall in the center of the hallway until the last man went down the stairs to the first floor. I quickly drenched the floors from the hallway all the way to the last open space.

I struck a match, tossed it on the floor and dipped before somebody was able to spot me. I darted back down the stairs like a wild animal. I refused to stop running until I was a block over and a few feet away from the getaway car.

I slid inside the whip with my heart beating in my ears. I had never done stupid shit like that. On the tail of anger, I gave in to my biggest fear. I just knew my life was about to be one big warzone. I was putting my momma in danger. I was reckless.

Seven minutes after I made it to the car, I saw a big ass fire blaze up from a mile away. I caught a glimpse of T-Max running towards the car like a Pit bull was chasing him. Instead of me waiting behind the steering wheel, he told me to keep my ass put in the driver seat. He wanted to do the driving in case somebody was hot on our trails.

"That's what the fuck I'm talking 'bout. That's how you do a fuckin initiation. Can't nobody change my faith in you. Cappo would be proud." T-Max pulled away from the block with a big ass grin on his face like he was my dad and just saw me walk across the stage to receive my diploma.

"Wasn't Cappo and Don homies though? I knew little about the whole gang banging, but I did once hear that my uncle and Don were cool until he took his last breath. Word had been the beef arrived whenever Gooch took over the gang. He wanted to bring forth a change and Don refused to bend a knee to be in alliance with old rival gangs. He wanted to keep things the old way while Gooch was all about evolving.

"Yeah they were, but he would still be proud of you stepping up to walk in his shoes. He asked me to watch out for his family and that's what I've been doing, even when it didn't seem like I was doing much of nothing." T-Max turned up the music with one hand while the other navigated the steering wheel. Numb by Rode Wave blasted over the speakers and I got lost altogether.

# OSIRIS

"Were you able to save anything?" Were the first words I let out when I laid eyes on Trever.

"Even with the amount I was able to save, I know we lost at least four hundred Gs." Trever shook his head as he viewed the firefighters still struggling to get the fire under control.

"Damn. That's fucking crazy bruh." I placed my hands on top of my head. The last time Don lost money, he went on the deep end and lashed out at everybody that was two steps too close to him. I was the one to witness it firsthand, and I wasn't ready to go back down that road. "Don isn't going to be happy about this at all. He sounded calm on the phone, but experience let me know how he is coming. Somebody is going to pay for all of this."

All Trever could do was continue to look at the fire that caused us to be in hot water. He was the one on duty at the warehouse, along with a handful of other people. Whether he was my right hand or not, it still wasn't going to save him from getting a taste of Don's anger.

"I swear to fuckin' God, I wasn't in on any of this. One minute I'm loading the truck because we have a shipment that goes out this week then the next, I see flames coming from upstairs." Trever thought convincing me that he was innocent was going to help him. Don was the boss, and whatever he decided for someone was what they received. He put down a lot of niggas over the years and would do it all over again.

"I want to believe you bruh; I do, but we both know I'm not the one that calls the final shots. If Don believes you're guilty of anything, you should already know I'm siding with him." I shot it at Trever how I saw it. He knew it would be stupid of me to go against Don's judgment. I did it once in the past and it came right back to bite me in the ass.

"Osiris, come on man, you know I would never fuckin' cross the boss. I swore to serve as your right hand and pledged my life to Don's team." Trever hit his hands together like he was ready to go toe to toe with a nigga. I was the last person he wanted to go there with. He knew better than to try some bullshit like that with me.

"Nigga I wish you would just calm the fuck down. Tell Don your side of the story and leave it at that. All that extra bitch shit isn't worth all the energy. Either way, he's still going to deal with it how he wants." I distanced myself from Trever. Without all the facts, I couldn't blame him for any of the shit that went down that night. Niggas were slick. If they saw you fucking off for even a minute they struck. I preached that shit to Trever; told him a handful of times to never be caught slipping. It be the niggas you least expect that hit you where it hurt. Enemies will go any length to make a hit on a crew. People that were in the game a while knew that shit.

"Is Don on his way?" Chief Miles asked. It didn't matter if it was home in Mansfield, Shreveport or across the fucking country, people knew Don. They vouched for Don at all cost. He was a businessman at best. With his dirty dealings under the table, he was a community man that helped the underprivileged neighborhoods. Law officials respected that as long as they were receiving whatever Don offered them to begin with.

"Yeah, I called him when I was on my way over here, so he should be pulling up any minute." Don taught me we didn't have to fear the cops if it was the cops who trusted us.

"Who could do something like this to Don?" Chief Miles asked.

"Some hating ass niggas is who, just have to find out which ones." I watched as the big blaze finally settled. I spent so many days in that warehouse making sure things went to plan. Relocating, making all that money back was going to take months. And within those months, Don was going to be riding everybody's ass.

"If you happen to run across any names, do shoot them my way. You know I don't mind locking people up who mess with Don's establishments." Chief Miles handed me a card like he did many times in the past.

"Yes sir, I sure will." I accepted the card like all the other times. Standing feet away from the car, I was able to see Lyric looking out the window of my car like she was in a maze. It hit me that she had no clue what Don was signing her up for. Every time she hopped out the bed in the morning, her life was going to be on the line for her team. She didn't deserve that. Lyric was too smart to be trapped trying to live up to Don's expectation of running his empire because she held his name. I was never a sexist, however, he was handing her a job that better suited a man. A job that most men died to have. If being a rapper is the dream she wants to chase then it's her dream and he should let her chase it.

If it wasn't for the bad news Mom Duke laid on me earlier that day, I never would've cared about Lyric wasting her life at Don's demands. I watched Mom Duke let go the things she liked doing over the years for us. She had dreams and aspirations in life, but she let it all go because of her family and now she wasn't sure how long she had left. Life wasn't something to be taken for granted. Standing there watching the warehouse flames slowly die down, I wished somehow it was possible to redo my past and let karma get my brother's murderer. Then I would have a choice, and maybe I wouldn't be tied to a gang until my dying day.

\* \* \*

"What's really going on, Siris?" Lyric stopped in her tracks on her way to the front door. She heard Don for herself; he didn't want her to know was going on to prevent her from worrying. It was his job to take care of all that mess that went on out there. I respected him for his decision to keep his family in the dark on the enemies that were trying to destroy his empire. However, they had a right to know that their lives were in danger too. Whenever Don put out a hit for somebody, he went after their families too. So, there was no doubt they were coming for his too.

"You heard him, he don't want you to know all that. Just believe we're going to get things under control," I said.

"Don't you think I deserve to know what's going on?" Lyric placed her hands on her hips. She viewed me like she would've set me on fire with her eyes if she possessed the power. Telling her about Don's business would've caused me to betray him, but to hold it from her was making me lose the trust I was working hard to gain. Proving to her that I was more than just Don's worker was what I aimed to do.

"The less you know, the better. I want to tell you; I do." Everything in my body was telling me to grab her in my arms and let her know that I wasn't going to let a damn thing happen to her. But the hood nigga that I was, I had to give her that tough love. Something she would learn to appreciate.

"But you can't because just like I said before, you're one of his minions. I don't know why I'm sitting here wasting my time on you. In the end your loyalty is with my pop, what he says goes. You're stuck with him, but I have a choice." Lyric reached for the door and I grabbed her arm to stop her. We were new to what we shared; not that we shared much to begin with, however, I was trying to build with her and show her that I could be the man she needed in her life. All the other niggas were only going to tell her what she wanted to hear while I didn't mind spilling the truth.

"Okay, so you want to hear from my lips that Don's enemies are closing in on him and they may be coming after his family. Then there you have it, that's all I fuckin' know." I released Lyric from the grip I had on her arm.

Once she was in the house safely, I dipped. On top of the problems I faced with somebody coming after Don, I was still sick about the news Mom Duke laid on me. Her results were like a ticking time bomb, and we both knew what the outcome could be. With all that was going on, I didn't get the chance to talk things over with Don about Mom Duke's condition, or the fact that I wanted to take some time off to be there for her. I put Don's need of me above anyone else's, but it was crucial now. The deck shifted and put me in a terrible spot. I was busy living the life of an outlaw, chasing the bag like money was the answer to all the problems. When all along, all she really wanted was for her children to be alright in the world and to make better decisions than our brother. Somehow, I stumbled right along that very path, and was sucked in by the man I owed my life.

"I heard you running around with Don's oldest daughter. Is it really safe to be pursuing her? I know you worked for him for a long time, but family sticks together. If you mess over that girl, hell will bust wide open on you. You know Don better than anybody." Mom Duke sat on the green, flowered couch that faced the front door.

"I thought you would be sleep. You must be feeling better?" I closed the door behind me.

"Don't try to change subjects on me. I stayed up because you need to hear what I have to say." Mom Duke kept her tone the same.

I took a seat beside her. With her dealing with health problems, I thought the last thing she would be worried about was who I was pursuing. She told me many times in the past that just because Don got me out of a tight spot didn't mean I owed him my life. Mom Duke was always focused on trying to get me to turn my heart and desire to God, but wasn't ready for all that. After all the things I did, I wasn't sure if God would have me anyway.

"Don gave me his blessing to be with Lyric. It's nothing set in stone, but I do hope that we end up together. Don has been good to me; to us. And you right, if I mess up with Lyric, he will put me down, but it's a risk I'm willing to take," I replied not shying away from my decision.

"I respect that son; I do. Just promise me, promise me, you won't be a slave to his authority forever. You have a big world ahead of you. There is so much more you can do other than slang dope and all the dirt he forces you to do for him," Mom Duke said. I don't know what made her words stick that night. Maybe it was because she was facing something that scared the both of us like hell, but they hit deeper that night.

"I wish I could, but I made an oath to Don and there's no getting out. He won't let me go." I shuffled to my feet and looked down at my Mom Duke with a heavy heart. "Don't worry about me. I'll be good."

# LYRIC

A few days had passed since the Shoe Toss and the fire that sent my pop into a rage. He stayed out late at night every day after somebody burned up his building. He made it home early in the morning to sleep for a little, then he was gone again. He kept telling us that everything was okay, and that he had it under control, but I knew he wasn't telling an ounce of truth.

I couldn't shake the feeling that he was dealing with something bigger than he led on. But with him dealing with whatever threats he was facing, he put it all aside to attend the funeral that was the talk of the hood.

"God makes no mistakes." The preacher started with the service.

I wasn't close to Mall; he was just a familiar face in passing over the years. We never hung around the same crowd. He was older than me by one year and a few months, so it was sad how he never received the opportunity to live out his entire life.

"Sometimes we question God, why he takes our children, our parents, sisters and brothers; our family. We say God never answers back, but it's not His job to make us understand His decisions. We must trust him enough to know that He's making the right decision." The preacher wiped the droplets of sweat from his forehead with the handkerchief he never put away.

Sitting there at the funeral made my stomach turn, because death wasn't ever something I thought about. I knew it was something that could happen, but it hit the block out of the trenches and took everybody by surprise. Especially me.

"Choir can you take us into a song please. Family please stand to view the body and friends please follow. I know it's not something we all gather for often, but we all know how it goes." The preacher closed the bible.

The first row stood first, closest to kin, then the other rows followed. The last time I viewed a dead body, I woke from nightmares twice a night for months. It seemed like the image would never subside.

"It's okay," Pop whispered to me. It felt good hearing him trying to talk me through a difficult time, because on a normal day we were forced to get through things on our own, due to him being so busy. Momma tried comforting us the best she could, but there was just something about the love of a Father that all girls longed for.

"Alright." I followed him to the casket to show our respect. My pop knew everybody, and not just in passing. He went to school with Mall's momma, and even served as the best man in his pop's wedding to his first wife. Showing his respect was something he held himself accountable for. My pop was the leader of the town, although he didn't sit in no kind of office fighting for the law. He was his own law.

I closed my eyes when I was near the casket, and never opened them to view the body. I couldn't put myself through that kind of torture again. I didn't want to see his face for nights at a time. I opened my eyes once I turned away from the open casket, then followed my family back to the fourth row that rested to the right side of the building.

"God," I murmured through a few tears. I never wanted to lose none of my family. It was a painful thought. It wasn't even the hood that caused his death; it was the company he kept. At least that's what everybody was saying on the block. Rumors had it, they decided to get high before a party and the driver lost control of the car. Everybody else walked away with a few bruises while he was slung right out of the car for not wearing a seatbelt. I half-ass realized why my pop was strict about me hanging out with people riding in their cars and shit.

"Glory, Gloryyy." The choir started another song as the last few people viewed the body.

I loved everything about music; I just couldn't bring myself to listen to it while sitting in that church. My mind was too wrapped around what was going on. What was really going on is a young man was only a few moments away from being laid in his grave.

After the service was over, everybody headed over to the graveyard to lay him to rest. The only thing that made my spirit lift was when I laid eyes on Beatz. It had been a while since I spoke to him in person. After dealing with Osiris and that whole mess at the warehouse with my pop, it felt good to see a face that didn't know what the fuck was going on behind the scene.

"I didn't think I'd see you here." Beatz walked up behind me in route to the car.

"Where else would I be? You know we all must pay our respects. It was terrible what happened to him. He was young, you know." I viewed Beatz; he was as handsome as they come. His five freckles that nobody seemed to notice made him ten times more attractive, too. And he was different. He was busy with music instead of beating the streets and slanging dope like everybody else. We were friends before anything else and that's how I wanted things to stay for a long time. Relationships ruin friendships. I saw too many close friends hook up, only to despise each other when the relationship failed. However, we somehow took that big ass chance regardless of the circumstance.

"That's true. You know I just thought maybe you'd be somewhere trying to make a hit." Beatz smirked, knowing I wasn't allowed to write music at home and the only studio I ever went to was the one he had in his back yard that he made out of a 70s portable trailer. The only place I ever wanted to be caught writing songs. He was my muse, literally. It made my conscious worsen to think that just last week I was out in the city with Osiris betraying what I shared with Beatz.

"That's not funny." Rolling my eyes, I positioned all my weight to one leg with my arms folded. Beatz knew how to ruffle my feathers. "You know my pop will murder me if he knew I was writing and shit."

"I still don't get it. You have mad talent out here, so why not let you follow your dreams?" Beatz dropped the joke to be serious for a moment. Although he was the only one to really hear me rap, he said it many times that I was destined for greatness if I just stopped listening to everybody else's take on my life and went after it.

"All that comes with the artist life is drugs, sex and more drugs. There are too many people who were in the limelight and committed suicide from the pressure and producers fuckin' the artist," I replied. I thought back on all the lectures my pop gave me about the industry, as if he lived the life. "That's his exact words."

"Man, I swear to God, I wouldn't let nothing happen to you out here. When we rise to fame, ain't nobody gonna pimp you out or turn you the fuck out. You gon' always be the muthafuckin' Hood Princess." Beatz hit his hands together to make his words stick.

"Hood Princess?" Pop stood behind Beatz in question.

"Excuse me; my mom is waiting for me. Nice chatting with you, Lyric. I'll be seeing you around on the block." Beatz knew he had to get away from me before he lost all the little favor he had in Pop's eyes. Not that it was much anyway. My pop blocked all the niggas who wanted me to their girl, even the ones who just wanted to be friends. Couldn't nobody change his mind that all boys were out for the same damn thing.

"Why you always do that?" I sighed.

"Do what?" Pop asked like he was completely clueless of what the hell I was talking about, but he knew what I was referring to.

"Every time a boy come talk to me, you have to cripple me. Like dang. I don't ever go nowhere, I stay home, I'm a good girl, so give me some space. What? Since he's not one of your Warriors he's not good enough?" I fussed. I tried my best to show respect to him; to be the girl he raised, but the older I got the harder it got to stay in control of my attitude towards him. "I need space." I stormed away from him and hopped in the car. It wasn't the perfect timing for me to be fed up with his strict rules, because we had just left the graveyard from showing our respect. I just couldn't shake it though. He irked my last damn nerves. He had no reason to treat Beatz like that. It pained me to even have to stress how different he was from all the other men on the block. He stayed out the way of the streets.

I felt like Pop was coming after me with the stunt I pulled in the public's eye. Thank God my momma stopped him before he opened the door to beat my ass like one of the niggas. He told me more than once that if I wanted to act like a nigga then he was going to show me how niggas get their ass beat. He didn't lie on several occasions either. He made sure he owned up to his words. He beat me one time until my whole body was numb while my momma just watched with tears running down her fair-skinned cheeks. Still, that didn't put any fear in my heart for Pop, because at the end of the day there is someone bigger, more malice than him that we had to face at the end of life. So, I had no reason to fear any man on earth.

"Don't. Not out here. Wait until we get home." Momma pulled on my pop's arm to make him stop. If he really wanted to, all he had to do was push her on the ground and open the damn car door. It wasn't like beating on her was a new thing. With his temper, he lashed out at everybody who got in the way of his rage. He blacked her eye one night when he came home late because she questioned him. Since that night, I never heard her ask him any questions about his whereabouts. She kept her mouth closed more than she needed. I figured it was in fear that he would beat her purple. I couldn't see myself bowing to a man like that, though. Never.

"Fine, but she going to think I'm wrong whenever we do," Pop replied.

"Don, you know she's not a little girl anymore. We as parents can only instill so much in our children. It's up to them to either live up to those values or to go in life to create their own." Momma removed her hands from his arm and hopped in the car.

All Pop could do was listen to Momma's advice until he was home with his family alone. He liked handling family issues in private, because he would never risk making himself look bad in public. If he beat our ass and we told somebody, he beat our ass again for telling. And if anybody got in the way of him trying to discipline his children, they felt his rage too.

The cops showed up at our house a few times after he beat us because the new neighbor, who wasn't familiar with him and the weight he pulled around town, called them. He talked to the cops like a Saint and they went on their merry way. After they were gone, he called one of his men to instill his kind of fear in the woman that lived next door. Ever since, she stayed out of his business. She even baked him cakes on a few occasions. It's insane what kind of fear a man can put in a person; how much power lied in one man's hand.

* * *

"Can I go to Cassie 'em house?" I asked time Pop pulled into the driveway.

"Yeah go ahead," Momma said before Pop was able to get his words out.

"Thanks Ma." I wrapped my arms around Momma from the back of the seat and hopped out the car on a mission. Dealing with my pop had to wait until after I got back. I dealt with his lectures for long enough and sat in the house until he was done instilling all his laws on me. Sat there and allowed him to kick me around the house without uttering a word too many times. His bullshit had to wait.

I texted Beatz to let him know I was on my way over to kick it with him for a while. I knew if I asked to go hang with him it wasn't going to happen, so whenever I wanted to chill with him and make some music I had to sneak behind my pop's back. Even our relationship remained a top secret.

When I made it past the first stop sign from my street, I saw Beatz's house from the distance. And before I took any more steps to get there, he'd already made his way to me.

"Damn were you running?" I shook my head and laughed at the thought of Beatz running. He wasn't like all the other dudes on the block who shot hoops to keep them sane. He wasn't seen with a basketball or football in his hand since middle school. He failed to enjoy sports activities, he enjoyed sitting in the studio trying to change up the music industry.

"Yeah. Shit, I regret it now." Beatz bent down to rest his hands on his legs.

"You crack me the fuck up. C'mon before my pop sees us or one of the Warriors." I grabbed Beatz's arm and led him up the street like I was trying to get a puppy to walk. Although his momma didn't support his dream to rock the mic, she allowed him his space to do what he loved because pulling him from his dreams was only going to cause problems. Problems she didn't need. If music was keeping her son out of the streets, then she kept her mouth closed. I loved that about her.

"I wish my pop could be like your momma. Although she doesn't support it, she still let you be." I slowed down to let Beatz walk ahead of me.

"You just have to show him that this is what you want and your heart is invested." Beatz opened the door to the studio and let me in first like the gentleman that he was. For his momma to be a single parent, she did pretty damn well raising her son.

"Yeah," I sighed.

Once we were in the homemade studio, Beatz did a few things with the computer, and then he opened the music software. "Aye, put these on."

I put the headphones on and before the beat was able to break down, I was already bopping my head while a rhyme, a sick verse, presented itself. If I wasn't good at anything else in life, I knew I could rock the mic with the sickest flow.

"All these girls tryna jack my flow bitch bow down you ain't like me hoe, bitch bow down you ain't like me hoe. Give a couple bars the sicker the flow. Louisiana spicy call me Creole Gumbo." I felt the beat, and I was ready to make some magic with Beatz. Although we hadn't been kicking it much in the past week, we were in there like we never fell off.

"Yoooo, I swear that's fire. Add a few more punch lines with some emphasis, and that rap gone blow." Beatz turned off the track. He viewed me for a moment. "Word on the street is that you riding with Osiris now. Isn't he cool with your pop and all that?"

I rolled my eyes. "Now here you go. Just because a few people saw me with Siris, doesn't mean a damn thing."

"Don't catch no attitude with me, I'm just telling you what they're saying. And I had no idea you two were alone together." Beatz turned his attention back to the computer. He'd been on my bad side a few times, and it was never a nice sight. "I guess he's the kind of man that Don approves. He's street smart, has a nice car, and rolling in bread. I don't have any of that shit."

"Beatz stop. I came over here to get away from my thoughts for a while. Can I just be in your company without all the extra? And how do you have the nerve to question me when you're still fuckin' with Pooh?" I propped my legs up on the milk crates that Beatz had in front of the sofa.

"I been rocking with you since forever; long before a damn Osiris stepped into the picture. I already told you I'm dropping Pooh. That ain't nothing but a word. But you, you putting yourself in a situation you ain't gon' be able to get out of." Beatz hadn't ever been that straightforward with me. He let me know how he really felt about things. I wanted to tell him about the whole Osiris situation myself, but the streets never failed to inform people.

"Why you have to make this an argument? I'm not even serious with Osiris. He asked me out on a date and I accepted it. Nothing happened. I swear nothing happened." I stood from the seat. I didn't want to talk about that with Beatz, but he just didn't understand. There was no doubt he was a good guy; it was who he was. If he finally ended things with Pooh and made us exclusive, he wasn't going to be able to handle me. I had a flip mouth, and sometimes got under people's skin without trying, but Beatz was too damn uptight. I wanted to slap my damn self because it wasn't until I started kicking it with Osiris that I realized that Beatz should've remained my friend.

"I have to go," I murmured.

Before I could open the door to let myself out, Beatz grabbed my arm and forced me to face him. The last thing I wanted to do was to hurt Beatz's feelings, or to bruise his ego. I never wanted him to think he wasn't good enough for me. The truth was he was too good for me. I was never deserving of a man like Beatz.

"When I look at you, I see this beautiful girl who has a good heart. You're perfect, and you're more than these streets will ever offer, Hood Princess." Beatz cuffed my face with his hands and brought me closer to him so that our flesh touched. He pressed his lips against mine while his heart thumped against the masculinity of his chest. It felt like he dragged me to a moment that was everything magic. I just wanted to stay there with him in that moment forever, where we didn't talk. We were perfect. No worries, nobody's heart ached. I was his girl; only his girl.

"I gotta go." I broke away from Beatz with tears in my eyes. It was crazy to me what the heart wanted, knowing it's not what it needed.

# LEX

Soon as we made it in the house, I grabbed Boni by the hand and led her into the room. She was the youngest of the three of us, four years under me. She and I shared the biggest age gap. Lyric always made excuses to leave than to deal with what was going on at the house. When we were alone, I never really heard her talk about the trauma we faced at home. I don't know if it made her tougher than me for not talking about it, or a coward for trying to cover it up.

"You have some muthafuckin' nerves to tell me what to do, to overstep my rules. If I say no, I mean fuckin no." I heard Pop through the walls of our room. Then following his yelling, I heard a dreadful cry that made my stomach tie in knots. I had a weapon, I could've shot him between the eyes if I wanted to; get rid of the monster out of our lives, although nobody saw him as such. I respected him like everybody else as far as the streets went, but it still didn't stop me from despising him at home.

"Cover your ears," I told Eboni. Then I walked over to my bed and retrieved my Glock from underneath the mattress. I took it off safety with nerves running throughout my body. I was tired of seeing my momma get her ass kicked around by the man that was supposed to be protecting us. I was tired of justifying his actions like he had a right to lay hands on her the way he did, or the way he slapped his daughters around and claimed it was for our good.

I walked out the room with my Glock tucked in the back of my slacks, I was still dressed in the clothes I wore to the funeral, and was prepared to ready the town to attend another on my pop's behalf.

"Bitch, I gave you this life, and I call all the fuckin shots. You just sit your ass up there and let me run this house. This is my house! Ain't no woman going to throw no kind of authority 'round while I'm here." Pop sat in the recliner while Momma sat on the floor in tears. His attention quickly turned to me like the angel told him I was present. "Take ya ass back in that room, can't you see grown folks are talking?"

"I'm tired of you putting hands on my momma like she some bitch out in the streets. You think what you doing is cool? What are you teaching us? What? To let a nigga walk all over us?" In my mind, those words sounded less harsh, but they were words that really expressed how I felt. I just wasn't expecting them to come out like that.

"Lex please, go back to your room. Go back to your room!" Momma yelled out through tears. I never opened my mouth to disrespect my parents; especially my pop. As a child, he put a certain kind of fear in me that made my stomach hurt at any sound of sudden commotion.

"What you said to me?" Pop raised from the chair with his eyes fixed on me. All of a sudden, my legs went weak, and my heart was beating so fast I could hardly breathe. The long-term fear was creeping right back into me with a simple damn warning. I wanted him dead and I had to kill him so we would no longer be burdened with his sick way of life.

"You heard me." I stood behind my words.

He took quick strides over to me, almost leaving his body behind. "Bitch, watch yo' fuckin mouth." He grabbed me up in the air by my neck and slung me across the room like I was a piece of paper.

"That's all you got?" I stood with my neck aching. Pain wasn't shy to overtake my body either, but I had something that could cause him more pain than his hands could ever cause me.

"Oh, you want to try me?" Pop was close to me. Close enough to yank me up and toss me across the living room like the first time. I was tired of all his bullshit though; tired of bowing down to his rules and tucking my tail. I respected that he was carrying the world on his shoulders by trying to stay on top, but that still wasn't a reason for him to do the things he did. None of it was a good enough reason for him to make his family fear him because of his own fear that one of us would betray him.

"Lex, please. Stop," Momma wailed. Her thing was that if she did right by him then he would do right by her. That he would eventually see her as a woman and not some punching bag; see her as his wife and not like she was a bitch on the streets. Her staying with him through all the abuse made me wonder many nights; like, was it love that kept her loyal to him or fear? I was young, but I knew a wife wasn't supposed to live in fear of her husband, or live in fear to stay safe and away from his wrath when things failed to go his way. I was always able to tell when the streets weren't going his way because he would lash out at Momma about the simplest things. The pain of loving a thug.

"Naw, I'm tired. All y'all do is fight. I'm tired of it. I'm tired of seeing it," I fussed, tears leaping out my eyes like they possessed legs. All I tried to do was protect my little sister from nightmares; from the same nightmares that used to punch me awake from my sleep at night. From the rumbling down the hallway, hearing our momma scream. Lyric couldn't protect me, so I was set on protecting the sibling underneath me the way I wished Lyric was able to do.

When I saw Pop ball his hands into fists, I grabbed my Glock. I brought it forward with my finger resting on the trigger. I fired a shot; a shot to scare him. The sound echoed in the house. The bullet went through the living room wall and to my guess, stopped at the last wall in the kitchen. "The next shot I won't miss."

"You…Did YOU try to shoot your own dad? You have the balls to pull a gun on me in my house?" Pop's voice was louder than music that played at the Hot Spot on the weekends.

"I didn't try to shoot you because if I did, you would've been shot on that try." I tucked my gun away and walked back into my room. Before I turned away, I saw a different kind of fear creep into my momma's eyes, and newfound hatred formed in Pop's. There was an enemy living under his roof. One he raised from an infant to a teenager. An enemy he created over the years of not giving a damn about nothing more than his fuckin' name. I was now a target on his back, and he would watch me more than he watched niggas in the streets.

When I made it into the room, Boni was laying on the bed with her hands over her ears. It hurt my heart to see her so afraid. To have to tell her to cover her ears whenever Pop decided to be ruthless behind closed doors.

"You can uncover your ears." I sat on the bed thinking on my fate. It would be by faith if my pop didn't have one of his Warriors to put a bullet between my eyes. Because knowing him, he was tough, but just not tough enough to kill his own daughter. At least I didn't think so. "Stay in here until things blow over. I'll be back later."

"Lex." Boni spoke in a shaky tone that made my heart drop. The fear was all bottled up in her. The fear I tried ridding her of since she was able to walk.

"Yeah?" I answered. My face was already a mess from crying, and another batch of tears was threatening to come out to make matters worse.

"Please don't die," Boni whispered.

"I won't." The stunt I pulled made me public enemy number one. It would be by the grace of God if I lived to see another day living under Pop's roof. It would've been foolish of me to believe that after pulling a gun on a man in his own home that things would blow over. Naw, I knew he was out for my blood. Shit wasn't over until he got the final say.

* * *

WYA? It's urgent! My fingers slid over the iPhone keyboard with the quickness. Hiding between anxiety and fear, anger crept out and made me lash out at the man who was a Saint in the public's eye. Michael told me earlier in the day that he wasn't going to be home; he was going to some group study with his pop. He mentioned his pop was stuck on making him fully converted into the faith. The only other person who knew me, like really knew me, was Lyric, so I sent the text to her. She'd been so in and out the house lately it was hard to keep tabs on her.

Walking from Beatz's studio; blah. I read Lyric's text at the speed of a light year. Starting from the stop sign leading to Circle Drive, I took off running, taking a short right to meet up with Lyric. Nothing was far on our block. Even the candy lady was right up the street. You couldn't get lost even if you weren't from the Eastside. The entire neighborhood was one big circle.

I don't know what happened, but I caught up to Lyric before she was able to meet me half way. I had to let her know what happened at home; about the dumb ass stunt I pulled. The one stunt that was probably going to make me meet God soon, if not the Devil.

"What happened? You straight?" Lyric asked, panic crippling her every word. Her mascara was a mess, and my face, I'm sure wasn't any better.

"They were fighting again, and I-I fired a warning shot at Pop. I think I fucked up, Lyric. I fucked up." The words shot out of my mouth like a volcano. My voice was barely recognizable to my own ears.

"Are you crazy? You shot at him! Why would you do something like that? That's stupid Lex, fuckin' stupid. You know how crazy he gets."

Lyric shook her head while it seemed like she was trying to hash a plan to save my ass, and come to my rescue after all these years. "Lex, you have to fix this. You have to beg for forgiveness. You have to fix this."

"How am I supposed to fix it when I broke the code? I'm his enemy. In his eyes I'm like the rest of the niggas on the streets that want to see him dead." I placed my hands on top of my head, breathing in shallow breaths. "I'm his enemy."

"You're hot his enemy, you're his daughter. His flesh and blood daughter. You made a mistake. It was a mistake, right?" Lyric refused to move her eyes away from me as her hands held onto my shoulder like she wanted to shake me for doing something so naïve. "Lex, was it a mistake?"

"I wanted to kill him." I let the truth slipped. I don't know if I was the only one that lived under Pop's roof that wanted him dead or not, but I had to live in my truth. The only mistake I made was not pulling the trigger.

"Lex, no. I understand he's not a very nice person to us sometimes, but he's our Pop. He's paving the way for us." Lyric looked like she was having a hard time finding a liking to her own words. I wondered how they tasted coming out of her mouth. "Family sticks together through it all."

"But you don't have to be a fool for family. You don't have to let your dreams go for family, or give your life to family, because we have a choice." I pushed past Lyric with anger drowning my soul.

*The only mistake I made was not pulling the trigger...*

## OSIRIS

"Look, I'm telling you, them niggas came out of nowhere. Like I told, Siris, one minute I was loading the truck then all hell broke loose. I would never cross you like that, boss. I swear on my sons' lives. You know me better than that." Trever sat in the chair with his hands tied behind his back. As my right hand, I expected more from his execution when I left him in charge. When Don left me at the spots to manage, I made sure the security stayed on the cameras and that the guards did routine checks. With enemies lurking at every corner, we had to stay on top of the game. As a member of Don's team, Trever should've known better.

"I don't want to hear any muthafuckin' excuses. You dropped the fuckin' ball, so what punishment do you think you deserve?" Don circled around the seat with his AK-47 held firmly in his right hand. I saw Don blow a nigga away more than once, and popped a gap between a man's eyes while he was pleading his case.

"I don't want to die, man. This is my team, my home. I wouldn't betray you. I swore an oath to Osiris, to the entire team. You think I want my family dead behind this shit? I don't." Trever said those words without a blink. He stared me right in the eyes. I knew when a man was telling a lie. He wasn't lying to Don, but it wasn't my place to convince Don of Trever's innocence.

"You fucked up though. People have to pay the price when they fuck up. You know this. Osiris, tell me the man you selected as your right hand knows that there's always a price to pay when you fuck up." Don looked over at me. I wasn't sure if I was supposed to answer or keep my ass quiet until he decided Trever's fate. "Do he fuckin' know or not?" Don was on ten that day, in a bigger rage than I ever witnessed.

"Yeah, he knows boss. Ain't that right nigga? You know the consequences," I said sternly.

"Okay, so since he don't want to open his fuckin' mouth to answer the question, what kind of punishment you think he should get?" Don shot another question my way. Knowing Trever, I knew he was going to hold that moment against me for not sticking up for him, but I couldn't dwell on that. He would've done the same damn thing if the shoe were on the other foot and he served as Don's right hand and I was the fuck up.

"Cut off one of his fingers, boss." It was the least torturous thing I could think of. He didn't deserve anything else. None of the things I figured was crossing Don's mind.

"You better thank Siris, because I was thinking about something worse. Like pluck the nigga's eye out or some shit." Don sat the AK-47 aside. He pulled out the pocketknife. "I would've shot him in the fuckin' eye. I hate letting a nigga off the hook that easy."

"Boss please," Trever begged. Making niggas pay was just too damn common for me. It's like every other day we had a nigga tied up to pay for his sins. Don instilled those morals in me since being a young nigga under his wings. It was clear that if I wanted to survive in the life of crime, I had to have some thick ass skin.

"Shut the fuck up!" Don grabbed Trever's hand. He slammed the knife into Trever's index finger. The only thing that filled the air was Trever's shouts for Don's mercy. But he knew he was already in the middle of receiving mercy, because things could've gone left for him real quick. A finger wasn't as important as an eye or leg.

"Ahhhh." Trever jerked his head from side to side.

"See, it wasn't that bad." Don showed Trever the finger. It never ceased to amaze me to witness the kind of thrill that filled Don when he was making someone suffer at his hand. Pain was who he was. He liked saying he was for right, but his actions made a lot of people question his motives. He had the entire hood scared to rat on him. I had to give it to him, though; he did reach his hand out to families that were in need of assistance.

"I would give it to you to have the doctors reattach it, but then all of this would be for nothing." Don dropped the finger on the floor. He stomped it and stomped it until he grew tired. He walked out the building and when he reentered, he held a gasoline jug in his right hand. He drenched the finger with gasoline then set it on fire. He made sure that Trever would live with the punishment. He would wake every day with a reminder to never drop the ball again. "Now get the fuck out of my sight."

Trever was gone before Don opened his mouth to say another word. With the heat Don brought down on him, I wouldn't have been surprised if he didn't show his face for a while.

"You better get your head out ya ass. This ain't something we should be taking light. There's a fuckin' threat. If they hit once, we best be expecting them again." Don wiped the pocketknife with the end of his Saints jersey, and walked out of the building without saying another word to me. Like all the other times, the world was on my shoulders. Don expected me to go crack the code like I had leads.

"Okay boss," I murmured. I had to get my shit together if I wanted to come through for Don like he came through for me. All the problems life threw my way had to be swept under the rug until things were looking better on the boss's end.

\* \* \*

Lyric was walking down Shallowhorn with her head down like she was having the worse day of her life. Before we got closer, I would've blown the horn and drove past her. Things weren't like before though. I wanted to know how she was doing, or what the hell she was doing way up the street alone knowing the streets were acting upon Don. On our crew.

"Need a ride?" I slowed the car down to a crawl.

Lyric looked over at the car and quickly dropped her head back down. She raised her hands to her face and dropped them again. "Naw, I'm good. You know I live right up the street. It's no big deal."

"So, we're back to that huh? You brushing me off like I'm nobody?" I said knowing she was going to come back with something smart out her mouth. Lyric was really the first female that ever tried to put me in my place. There was no fear in her step or any kind of weakness in her tone. "I thought we were better than that?"

"Nigga why you always bugging? It's either your way or no way. Damn. Stop the car," Lyric snapped like so many times in the past. The only thing that was different about her reply this time is that it sounded like she wanted to be next to my crazy ass.

"You must live off attitudes." I said once she was situated. The drive from that street to hers was only two minutes tops in a car, so I had to shoot the shit quick then drop it until we were really able to be next to each other. "Your lil' boyfriend done pissed you off or some?"

"My attitudes are based on people and their bullshit. And for the record, I don't have a damn boyfriend." Lyric folded her arms without saying any more words. The next fifty-nine seconds were cold. She hopped out the car time I pulled up into the driveway. The dedicated Warrior in me knew I had to get up the street to see my cousin for his helping hand in bringing Don's enemies to the front row. Jab was smart with computers and shit. Even with the niggas wiping the cameras clean, there wasn't a doubt in my mind that he was going to be able to recover the footage. But the lover in me wanted to chase after Lyric to see what was eating her alive like that. It was a beautiful day, she was a beautiful girl, and she didn't want for a damn thing. So, I put the car in park and hopped out to chase after her ass up the driveway.

"I don't even get a *thank you*? What kind of shit is that?" I blocked her from moving past me. Her ass wasn't 'bout to go anywhere until she spoke to me like she had sense. She had to learn to respect me. I wasn't those other clowns out there who had to lick her ass. Yeah, sure enough her dad was my boss, but still I wasn't some nigga who was scrapping to make ends meet and shit. I was serving as her dad's right hand. I deserved respect, and I mean lots of fucking respect.

"Thank you for bringing me home," Lyric sighed as she looked at me with bucked eyes. "Are you happy now?"

I grabbed her closer to me as I planted a kiss on her pink, plump lips. I don't know what it was about Lyric that made me intoxicated, but I couldn't get enough of whatever it was. "Lyric, why won't you just let your guards down for me? I will protect you to the best of my ability."

"Have a nice day Siris." Lyric turned away from me without any further words. I had to give it to her, she wasn't an easy cookie to crumble at all, but I knew if I really wanted her, I had to show her different.

After I left Lyric alone, I headed over to Jab's spot like I intended before my eyes fell on Lyric walking up the street. It was three cars parked in front of his house when I pulled up into the driveway. I kept my circle small, but Jab kicked it with everybody. There wasn't a reason for him to watch his back for snake ass niggas because he stayed out of the limelight of crime. My Mom Duke even fussed that I should be more like him, but I couldn't. My life was sorted out since I was a lil' nigga.

"Look what the sun baked up," Qunence said as he reached out to give me dab. Back on my old block, I used to run with Qunence and the south side crew. When I was out with revenge on my heart, he gave me all the info on the nigga who took my brother's life. He supplied me with the Glock and everything. Time Don saved my life, I cut ties with the Southside. I couldn't ride for them anymore. They didn't hold me to it either because they knew that Don done things that nobody else could.

"Damn bruh, it's been a long ass time. We up here acting like we live in a big city and shit, when all we have to do is ride ten miles up the street to kick it." I gave him dab, grabbed him in a brotherly embrace, and turned my attention to Jab who was to the left of me shooting dice.

"Nigga, you already know what's up. Let's get to work," I said.

"Hold on na, let me get this bread up real quick." Jab brushed me off and focused back on the task at hand. It wouldn't be the hood if you didn't see a nigga shooting dice on the porch or sitting out in the yard playing dominos. Eastside had its difficult times, but the crime rates were low. People knew which lines to never cross if they wanted to stay on the block.

"So, when are you going to start your own team? You know all the outs and ins. Shidd, I say stop being a middleman and get you a middleman." Qunence handed me a fifth of Henny. I messed with the liquor on the regular, but I had to stay sober since the shit happened back at the warehouse. One slip-up could've caused hell to open wide.

"I'm not even looking to do any of that. On the real, Don is true to the muthafuckin' game. Being with a crew like his has benefits, and if I try to go out and get my own, all I'll be doing is making enemies on the streets." I accepted the bottle of whiskey, and took a sip then put it away. If it was a few years earlier, I would've chugged the entire bottle. It wasn't like that back then because none of us wanted to be looked at as a bitch, especially me. But things changed, and I had no desire to look a certain way in nobody's eyes. What they believed about me was on them. Their opinions didn't make me and it sure as fuck didn't break me.

"Loyalty has a way of putting fear in a man's heart." Qunence downed the rest of the whiskey in the bottle without a rumble.

"There's no fear in my heart. I never feared anybody. Yeah, I know what my boss is all about, but it's not fear the keeps me loyal. It's the fact that I owe him for everything he's done for me. That's just showing my fuckin' gratitude, bruh. You feel that?" I stood behind my words. Old homies or new homies, none of them were going to turn me against the one man that had a heart of gold in my eyes. Don was a true muthafuckin' OG.

"Alright, let's get to work." Jab punched me in my shoulder as he retreated into the house. "This won't take long. Y'all stick around while I take care this for my cuz."

"Aight nigga," Qunence said.

I followed Jab down the narrow hallway down into his room. He still had Tupac posters and collectible cars that he rebuilt. There were a few *Playboy* magazines spread over the bed. I didn't think people still looked through those things, especially not Jab. The shorties were after him. He never had a hard time getting pussy, so the magazines threw me for a loop.

"Don't mind the mess; I was in the middle of spring cleaning when those niggas popped up on me. I remember getting these from one of the OGs up the block when I was a lil' nigga. Boy the fuckin' memories." Jab pulled the desk chair and took a seat.

"I was just 'bout to say, 'cause I know you weren't still jacking off to those bitches." I slid the magazines to the side and took a seat on the edge of the bed. It felt like old times being in there like that. When we were young teenagers, we used to stay kicking it inside of his room smoking, looking through magazines and sneaking girls through his mom's back door.

"Naw, I'm not deprived anymore." Jab let out a light chuckle. He fired up the computer, and looked over his shoulder at me. "I'm trying to recover wiped footage, right?"

"Yeah, that's correct. Some niggas burned down one of the warehouses. Right before they made the hit, they made sure the video footage was wiped." I handed the hard drive over to Jab. He didn't hesitate to get to work either. I just kept quiet and allowed him to work his magic.

## BEATZ

Right after Lyric left me to deal with my thoughts, Pooh called and asked to come over. Hell, with Lyric falling for Osiris, I was in desperate need of a distraction. From the way Lyric spoke her words and the force behind them, she was considering letting what we had burn to ashes.

"Why you not looking at me?" Pooh asked. I used to love the way she spoke her words. The way that one gold tooth made her look like Halle Berry from B.A.P.S. Now I just wanted to close my eyes and pretend she was Lyric.

"It's just a lot on my mind." At least I spoke on some of the truth. There was a lot of things on my mind. I was officially a 211 Viper in the arms of no return. I was an enemy to most gangs in passing; the Eastside Warriors being the prime rival.

"Well, let me ease your mind, babe. That's what you want? For me to ease your mind?" Pooh removed herself from the seat and positioned herself on her knees in front of me. Head used to make my dick shoot up at short notice, but it didn't do a damn thing while she was on her knees. My heart, my lust, none of it belonged to Pooh.

"Just get up. We need to talk." I pushed her hands off my lap. Since becoming honcho of 211 Vipers there was a lot flooding my brain. Then on top of that, my girl was falling in the arms of a real thug, not some square that forced himself to become one.

"Okayyyyy then." Pooh raised from her knees. She looked down at me with her hands resting on her hips. It looked like she would slap me upon hearing anything she didn't want to hear.

"I feel like we should take a break. I already know you been doing your thing out there on the streets with other dudes. It's time I have some time to do mine," I said, looking right up into her eyes without an ounce of pity in my heart. Any bitch that beat the streets should've seen a day like that coming. Wasn't no nigga dumb enough to stay with a trifling woman forever. Pooh had a whole lot of growing to do. We both did. She needed time to figure out what she wanted out of life. Like if she really was into being just another bitch on the streets getting tossed around, or if she wanted to be with one man exclusively.

"You breaking up with me? Like, are you even listening to your damn self right now? Since you started hanging out with that bitch, you been acting strange. I knew it was coming. What? She gave you a lil' pussy now you sprung?" Pooh rolled her neck 'round what seemed like a thousand times as she spoke.

"If you ain't know, Lyric and I have been friends since the sandbox. And according to my calculation, that's way before you and I even started talking, so don't stand up here and act like she's new in my life," I replied.

Pooh balled her hands into fists, and punched me dead in the nose before I was able to react. Pain instantly traveled from nose to my head. For a moment, all I saw was stars wrapped in darkness. "Fuck you, Beatz!"

I was raised to not put my hands on a woman, but all those values went straight out the door that night. She had me for the wrong nigga. I wasn't any of the men she fucked whenever she pleased, and I sure as hell refused to sit up there and allow her to walk out after almost breaking my nose. That was my thing; some women put their hands on niggas, but played the victim whenever they felt the same energy they douched out.

"Bitch!" I leaped from the couch, wrapped my hands around her neck, and slammed her into the wall, causing all the records I had hanging to fall like we were in the middle of an earthquake. I couldn't stop tossing her around the studio if I wanted to. Rage filled my lungs, making me drown in a dark ocean. I never wanted someone to pay so bad for crossing me. For trying to make me look like a damn fool out there on the streets after being nice for damn near a year. Fucking other niggas for money instead of going out to get it on her own or coming to me. I wasn't a rich nigga, however, I was able to fund nails and hair if that's what the fuck she wanted the money for.

"Oh my God! Stop! Please stop," Pooh wailed, balling up in a corner in desperation for me to stop beating on her. I wasn't set on stopping; that's what she wanted. All the bitches on the block flocked to thugged out niggas who didn't give a fuck about knocking their jaw loose, and treating them like a dog, so I insisted on giving her what the fuck she wanted.

"Naw, that's what you want right? You want a nigga who's gone beat your ass, kick you around, and make you feel low. Right?" I jerked her up by her arms, forcing her to stand. I ripped the purple tank she wore, exposing her breasts. It was her fault she failed to wear a bra. I told her plenty of times in the past to cover up more, but she brushed my words off, and took me as a joke. I was willing to show her just how big of a joke I was. "You like it right?"

I raised up her skirt, her pussy exposed. She was there to fuck, suck dick, and do what she did best, so I utilized her at what she was good at. I wrapped my hands around her throat like the first time I snapped out on her, and pressed her back against the wall with her right leg slung over my forearm while I pulled out my dick somehow in the process. I went into her like I was boning a slut on the streets. Eleven months of trying to get her to see her worth, three-hundred and thirty-four days I fought to show her different from what she was used to in a man. I supported what she wanted to do, even when I thought it was a terrible idea. She just wanted a simple life; get a job at McDonald's and figure her life out later. I failed to listen to my momma when she told me to steer clear of Pooh. I gave her the benefit of the doubt.

"Stop Beatz. Please, I'm sorry." Pooh cried out to me like that was going to make me feel sorry for her. I didn't. I violated her in more ways than I was able to count on both hands. I was a monster with her; a person that was a stranger in the mirror.

* * *

"Quiet down, quiet down." T-Max spoke over the roars that the 211s were making on my behalf. I hadn't been in their presence since we hit Don's warehouse, and made him lose a shit load of money. He was going to be feeling that loss for months. "A lot of you questioned my decision to crown him honcho. You say, after thirteen years it didn't matter if a man didn't have Alejo blood running through his veins; that any man could step up to the plate. I call bullshit, because Beatz did something we never thought to do."

"What now? We just pull from under Wayne's leadership with the Serge Gs? Having a honcho over 211s means we no longer have to bow to his rules." Phons talked rough at T-Max.

Serge Gs was one of the most violent gangs around, second to the Eastside Warriors. Honestly, in my book, they ranked at number one because Don had his men in line. They never did shootouts on the block or blasted in broad daylight. Don was a clean man when it came to gang violence; he did it under the table. Jacked niggas up and banished them. He looked out for the community in the process. He built up around the town. That's how I wanted to lead my gang, but make them better. We were going to rise.

"We're going to deal with that. Wayne already knew that this day would come. He never had rightful claims of this gang; he just put us under his protection due to the alliance. We don't have to bow to any rules anymore. We will wear our tats out freely and put our jackets back own. This is our time to rise." T-Max threw up the 211s gang sign, and the men standing outside followed his lead.

"You sho' doing a whole lot of talking. Let the lil' square honcho speak." Phons was still breathing down my neck. Although the others accepted me with open arms after I was officially initiated, he was still trying to find a way to shame me to the gang. Whatever respect he held for the Alejos' family was long gone. It was no secret he wanted the honcho position, however, my uncle sealed his family's name in blood on the throne. "How are you going to deal with a nigga like Wayne?"

"How do you deal with anybody? You see, you're too used to rivals and not enough peace. Wayne and I, along with T-Max, will chop it up, stand on mutual grounds, and reinstate our alliance with Serge Gs like old times. We're not trying to start a bloody war with them. We're just in no need to be under his wings anymore." I spoke those words like I knew what the hell I was talking about. I didn't know what it was, but I couldn't sleep at night anymore. My mind was always on the 211 Vipers and what I could do to put us back on top. Even songs weren't coming to me like before. I was stuck trying to show the streets that honchos weren't made out of gang violence, but we were birthed. "For the last thirteen years, they've stood beside us as brothers and we will continue to do so with a new honcho on the throne."

"Nigga, Wayne ain't gon' chop it up with you," Phons chuckled, like I was one big joke. If I was going to survive as honcho, I had to show them not to cross me, or make me look like a big joke. Phons was going to bend the knee to my leadership or be banished.

I grabbed T-Max's AR-15, and aimed it at Phons like I knew what the fuck I was doing. Knowing damn well if I would've fired the gun, I probably would've missed, but there was no way I was going to look weak in front of my new crew. "Nigga, you better fall in line or I will blow your fuckin' brains out. Now kneel to your new honcho."

T-Max stayed quiet, I felt his eyes on me though. All the other niggas had already bent the knee; I just wanted to make Phons show his respect so that we were on the same page.

Phons placed his hands in the air in defeat. "All hail the new muthafuckin' honcho." He kneeled and gave me the respect I deserved.

"Now that we're all on the same page, let's take over these streets." I threw up the gang sign and everybody followed my lead like they did T-Max. The streets weren't ever going to be the same.

After I dismissed myself from the crew, T-Max and I headed to the space that I now knew as my office. Whenever a nigga wanted to chop it up with me, they were invited inside of my office space. Unlike the last time, I sat behind the desk as the big dog while T-Max sat in front of me. He was my right hand; right hand to the 211 Vipers. We were a team.

"I was afraid you would use it for a second." T-Max fired up a blunt.

"Then we better get those shooting lessons out the way." I chugged the shot of rum like a boss. It burned like before, but it made me feel official. I felt stronger. A new man was birthed.

# LYRIC

"Naw, hold on. Let me have a word with you." Pop stopped me in my tracks.

"Godd," I sighed. All I wanted to do was leave out the house without having to hear his sermon. He was always talking to me about the company to keep and the family name I had to uphold with my life. After what I pulled back at the gravesite, I was surprised he didn't snatch me up like a ragdoll. And, with the beef that lied between him and Lex, he was on my case more. Lex wasn't the kind of person to apologize if she felt her actions were justified. And, though she never wanted to admit it, she acted like Pops more than anybody. They were right in their own ways, and an apology never presented itself.

"Aye na, don't be taking His name in vain. You already know how I feel 'bout that shit." Pop grabbed a Newport from his pocket as he retreated over into the living room.

"My bad." I was on his heels. All of my friends were out of school. Some weren't in school to begin with. The first day of break, everybody was trying to find something to get into. The streets were packed with people playing street ball and racing each other like they were on the track field, while others were doing tricks on bikes as if the road were a BMX park. After all the shit I had going on in my personal life, dealing with my pop holding secrets and he and Lex at each other's throat, I was in desperate need of a fun day.

"I already know what you 'bout to say," I said.

"That's not the point..." Pop trailed off when he heard the screen door open. "Aye, bring ya ass in here too. You need to hear this." Lex closed the door back and drug her feet over the carpet. Since we were knee high, he was instilling skills he thought we would need to survive long after he was gone. Then we had a job to do right by his name; it was his legacy we had to protect. I was tired of hearing that shit all the fucking time. I had dreams that didn't fit into the life he was trying to force on me. The other day I was trying to speak sense into Lex's head about seeing Pop in a different light than an enemy, but he had control over our lives like we were slaves. The shit was growing old, quick.

"Y'all know people look up to me out there and they expect more from my children; my family. You can't be doing the shit those other children are doing." Pop started with his long-winded conversation. I was already rolling my eyes and he had just started. Since turning eighteen back in January, I wasn't referring to myself as a child. I was legal; done with school and with dreams that he frowned upon.

"I'm not a child," I corrected.

"As long as you're under my roof, eating the food your momma prepares, and wearing the clothes I bought on your back, you're a child. And, you will forever be my child. Understood?" Pop finally lit his cigarette.

"Yes sir." I backed down like all the other times in the past. I was wishing for the day that I would be able to face him; stand up to his face and tell him that I wasn't going to follow in his footsteps.

"Now as I said, don't be out there fuckin' up my name. I have respect and my family will be respected. My children will be something major in life, so all that sleeping with these lil' nasty niggas, keep your legs closed. Drugs is out of the question and when an elder asks you a question, you answer with respect." Pop blew smoke through his nose. "And Lex, that stunt you pulled the other day will never happen again. Won't no child of mine threaten me. Understood?"

"Then stop doing the shit you do," Lex snapped. I don't know what jumped into her to make her act out like that, but Lex had been on ten since the other day. She was snapping people up without any pity or fear.

"Oh okay, you want it to be like that huh? You sho' you want those problems? You want to be my enemy for real? Alright you got yourself an enemy." Pop stared at Lex like he was about to let hell rip on her.

"You're both dismissed," Pop said. He was a month too late to tell me to keep my legs close. Beatz and I had been having sex whenever we wanted, or more like whenever I was able to sneak around. It was too bad he and I weren't seeing eye to eye since Osiris popped up into the picture.

"Yes sir," I said.

Lex was the first to start on her way out the house and I was right behind her. I was in a hurry because my friends were waiting for me. I was definitely the showstopper. Boys flocked to my feet, but many of them shied away because of my pop and how crazy he would get whenever someone tried to approach me.

Once I was far enough from the house, I tied my shirt up in the back so my flesh was visible, then I cuffed my basketball shorts up an inch higher.

"You gon' get ya ass beat if Pop crazy ass see you." Lex wasn't a stranger to the way I went against our pop's wishes. She had her own misbehavior moments. She snuck out of the house sometimes too. And hell, since we left the house she was ruled as an enemy to our pop.

We had a bond though; we weren't about the snitching life. Everything that we did stayed within the walls of our rooms. We had a true sisterhood. Regardless of the friends I had, my sister was always the first person to know my business. And that's why I was going to have her back once Pop came down on her head.

"Girl shut up, damn. You always in somebody else's business. He ain't gone see me." I continued on my path up the street until I reached Monique and Cassie's house.

"Just keep all eyes on you, though. It makes my life a whole lot easier," Lex smirked as those words oozed from her mouth.

"Yeah, whatever." I brushed Lex off. I had better things to do than stand up there and argue with Lex, knowing damn well she was doing it to be entertained by me.

"Ayyeee. Bad bitch alert." Cassie retreated from the driveway to the road.

"You see it hoe." Sometimes I had to look in the mirror to see who the hell I was for concrete sure. Back at the house with my family, I was respectful and never really cursed. But let the streets tell the story; I was a completely different person.

"You heard about Beatz breaking up with Pooh?" Monique joined the clique in the road then we headed up to the neighborhood hangout that was only a few blocks over. The spot Pop had built for the neighborhood about five years ago. Although he was still living in the hood he grew up in, he was in a position to give back. If he wanted, he could've easily moved us to some gated community, but to him, the Eastside of Mansfield was home. The town was small and the crime rates were low. He told us over and over that he wanted us to never grow up like we were better than anybody because of where we lived.

"He was too good for her anyway. She's a slut." Although Beatz and I weren't getting along, I would always be the first one to speak highly of his name. We shared the same love for music, but Beatz always said my love was greater than his. I just had to take charge of my dreams and stop allowing people to tell me what was right for my life. Whenever we linked, we made magic in the studio. Magic we couldn't let the world hear because my pop wasn't in any favor of it. And since a month ago, we were making magic in other areas too.

"Downright slut, she done sucked every nigga's dick on the block." Cassie joined in on the conversation. "I heard she was pregnant before too, she got rid of the baby somehow. I know she ain't see a doctor though."

"Nasty ass. Her mother on that shit too, so you know that girl just doing whatever she wants," Monique replied.

Once we made it to the hangout, Lex went her separate way to join her friends. She wasn't the type to do girl gossip; she preferred chopping it with the fellas.

"I'll catch up later," Lex shouted across the distance.

"Big facts bitch," Cassie said.

"Aye Lyric, Mr. Don finally let you off that leach?" It seemed like the entire basketball court stopped playing basketball when Trey yelled out at me. Trey was the supposedly smart kid on the block. He hung around a tough crowd, but he kept his head in his books because his momma never tolerated bad grades. While on the other hand, his older brother had an entire life ahead of him, paid for in full at the University, but he got ahold to the wrong drugs and was never the same.

"Nigga, I'm not never on no leash. The fuck you thought this was?" I shot the shit back at Trey. All the joking and shit was part of everybody's day. None of us ever took it to heart. Things were different whenever crews from the Southside wanted to ride up on our hood, members of the 211 Vipers, especially. Their entire crew was nothing but trouble. Whenever they ran into anybody from the Eastside, they wanted to start a fight, so nobody joked with them. We kept it a buck and kept it moving.

"Alright, good girl. We already know what it is." Trey dropped the lil' conversation and started a game of basketball. I swear those niggas loved to show out when me and my girls were around. They would nearly run each other over, throw elbows and all kind of shit to look like they were the MVP of the game. Truth be told, I wasn't into no damn basketball players.

"Why you won't get on him?" Monique asked, out of the blue.

I cocked my head to the side while raising my left eyebrow. "Get the fuck on who?"

"On Beatz, he seems like a good dude. He sure comes running whenever you call his damn name. I think it's a match made in heaven," Monique said, like she knew Beatz like the back of her hand. She never really hung out with him or knew the type of person he was. I knew the fuckin' streets talked, she just didn't have a right to tell me who she thought was best when she was out there trying to search for the next best thing.

"Lyric ain't 'bout to talk to no Beatz when she got the hots for Osiris. That nigga is like a trustworthy friend of her family. She riding for that nigga like Faith rode for Biggie." Cassie put her two cents in where it wasn't needed.

"Bitch, I'm gone need you to mind your business." I played off my nerves with a light giggle. She knew I never went for a bitch being all up in my business like that. I told her to stay clear of Osiris because I knew he was feeling me and I didn't want her to end up getting her feelings hurt. When a nigga caught feelings for me, it was hard for them to shake back.

"I'm just saying, look like you wanted to kick my ass when I was trying to get all over that." Cassie took a seat on the picnic table with Monique following her lead.

"I'm not even going to speak on it any further." I dropped the conversation before it could go any further. Just as I was about to take a seat beside Cassie, Beatz walked into the hangout with a few boys I never saw around the block until then. I had to double check myself; I mean, Beatz hung out, but he never really just showed up at the hangout like that. He was too busy making beats and writing songs.

"We just spoke his ass up." Monique was the first to speak on Beatz's sudden appearance. "Beatz, over here."

"No, no, no," I said. I was too late to tell Monique to shut the hell up and let him be with his friends. He was already walking across the concrete over to us.

# LEX

Lyric and her friends were cool; just wasn't the crowd I felt comfortable associating myself with though. Plus, Monique was too over the top for me and had done any and everything for attention. In my eyes, she of all people wasn't a friend to Lyric. She was always trying to cripple Lyric's spotlight.

Like on usual days, I found myself catching up with Michael, the only nigga that was allowed to really know me. We never made anything official between us, but we were tight; we were more than friends. I loved him, being around him, just everything about him. We were young though; too young to even know what it was we were feeling for each other. I knew a few girls who thought they were in love at my age, only to come up pregnant and the niggas hit the ground running and never looked back. So, I knew not to get my whole heart vested only to be let down in the end. Even if my heart thought it knew he was different.

"There she is, the one and only Lexis Danielle Cotton," Michael yelled as he made his way down the driveway. Only he could yell my entire name out without me giving him a punch to the throat. Michael was overly playful with me. He always tried making me smile; it was his thing. He had a heart of gold. I knew that the day we first started hanging out, and the day he took off his shoes to give to a student who was being bullied for his.

"Nigga, you stay causing a scene." I looked around to see who all was listening to his crazy ass out there. Since school let out, the streets were packed and the messy ass people were always in search of their next topic to discuss. Unlike most people, I didn't mind being the talk on anyone's tongue, because at the end of the day it was all only gossip. Truth be told, every fuckin' body gossiped whether they owned up to that shit or not.

"Aye, that's why you cool with me though." Michael draped his arms over me. We walked along the sideway with our arms around each other. Ere to what happened between Pop and me, I would've never been seen walking the sidewalk like that with Michael. I was so bent on upholding the values, but things changed.

"Big facts lil' nigga." I giggled.

"This lil' nigga have a big dick." Michael loved talking 'bout the size of his manhood. It was something that grew old fast. I couldn't hold it against him; it was what most niggas did to feel like they were on top of the world or some.

"Yeah, whatever you say," I replied.

We ended our walk up the street next to Moomoo's grandma house. Second to Michael, Moomoo was my good friend. Nothing close to a best friend, just a good friend that I was able to kick it with without the fear of being judged. To be honest, I never really considered anybody as a best friend, especially not another bitch. Girls were too damn wishy-washy for me. I was friends with mostly dudes, really acquaintances. They kept up way less drama; more violence, but less drama. That's what I preferred.

"Let me find out y'all together." Moomoo joined us on the sidewalk.

Since everybody was at the hangout, we were heading back in that direction.

"Who is that?" Moomoo pointed towards the classic black, dark tinted Monte Carlo pulling up on the block. Pop told us which cars to watch out for since were children. If they crept too slowly, we move our ass out the way. If the windows were too dark, we get our ass out the way and take cover. And, if a car sped up down the block and we saw windows roll down, we try our best to get to safety.

"I don't know." We hadn't had any drive-bys since I'd been alive, so instead of ducking and dodging, I ignored my pop's teaching. It was a pretty day out, and I was focused on making my way back to the hang out to kick the summer off right.

"So, neither one of y'all brought a blunt?" Moomoo walked with her left hand on her hips while she swung side to side. At sixteen, she was stacking in all the right places. I mean, bad bitch from the head down. And her bleached blonde hair brought out her caramel skin complexion even more. "I need something to take the edge off."

"Out of luck. My dad confiscated all my weed; I mean all of it. Then he made me go to his bible study thing; had some of his brothers try to preach sense into me. I can't wait until I'm legal and can move the fuck away yo'. He be cramping me." Michael talked with his right hand. It was a thing that niggas from the hood picked up on. It seemed like they all talked with their hands whenever they discussed some deep shit. "I don't know why parents can't understand that we have our own lives. Just because he converted faiths and wants to be closer to God or whoever he calls on, doesn't mean I have to be part of it."

"I feel you," Moomoo replied.

"Aye, hold up bitch." I heard a boy say from behind us, and peered around to see what was going on. There were a few people walking up and down the sidewalks in both directions. "You heard me lil' Eastside bitch." On that cue, I stopped in my tracks to see if the nigga was talking to me or Moomoo. I never had problems in our neighborhood.

"Who the fuck are you talking to?" I reached to the back of my pants in an attempt to get my Glock, but it wasn't there. Somehow, my ass was rushing and accidentally left it. "You better have some respect nigga before I get some Warriors on your ass."

"Oh, yeah. You Don's lil' bitch of a daughter. I'll bust a cap in your ass for him. Drop your body at his door as a present." The boy couldn't be any older than Lyric. His face was mad familiar, but it was my first time seeing him on our block. It had to be somewhere out at the store or just in passing. It was never on our block, though. I couldn't believe I put myself and my friends in a situation like that when I knew better. When the all black Monte Carlo bent the block, it was a sure sign of trouble. I should've stuck with what I was taught instead of thinking that all the values were paranoia that my pop wasn't able to get over.

"Aye, watch your muthafuckin' mouth speaking to her like that. I don't know who the fuck you think you tryna to disrespect, but the shit stops here." Michael removed his arm from around me. He and the boy was damn near chest to chest until the boy pulled out a Maxim 9 suppressed pistol. Being raised by a honcho like my pop, a person couldn't help but to know all about guns. Guns were his best friend, second to his right hand.

"Get out the way bitch," the boy said to Michael. I tried to move Michael out the way myself, because if they were after me, it had nothing to do with him. My trouble was my own to deal with. I didn't need him being a hero on my account.

"You get off this block hoe." Was the last words I heard Michael say before his body fell to the ground. It was like everything after that moved in slow motion, like I was standing in the middle of a movie scene or something. The boy ran off along with another boy who was waiting next to the Monte Carlo a few feet away.

"Nooooo," I screamed so loud, almost busting my own eardrum.

# LYRIC

*It* took him a good two minutes before he and his friends made it over to us. Beatz gave Cassie and Monique dab then the boys that were with him followed his lead. He skipped me. He just went right in talking to Cassie 'em like I was a ghost. I couldn't blame him, he had to still be in his feelings about the whole Osiris situation I had going on.

"Keep trying to get y'all to come over to the studio. I'm trying to do more collabs with local artists for a showcase that I'm working on hosting." Beatz talked to Monique and Cassie like he was cool with them for an eternity. He never spoke to me about a damn showcase, so I knew he had to be popping off, or he just somehow came up with the bullshit overnight. I wasn't even sweating it.

"That'll be cool, just give us the date and time. Me and my girls will come over there and wreck the mic." Monique spoke on us like she was the reigning leader. I worked on my own time, and wrote my own songs. They knew what was popping with me. We weren't any official group. My solo career was going to take off quicker than any group.

"That's a bet." Beatz finally turned his attention me; not like I cared if he did or didn't. "Why you being so quiet?"

"I'm just trying to figure out this new Beatz," I replied.

"New?" Beatz questioned while he looked around at his homies as if they were going to back him. He was with a group of new niggas that weren't from our hood, and that made me uneasy in the worst way.

The moment I was about to summon up a reply, my phone started going off, and Lex was running across the concrete washed down in sweat.

"Hello," I answered.

"You and your sister need to get in the car with Siris." Pop sounded like he was running. My entire body went cold; it felt like my blood drained from my head down to my toes. I was done. I knew some bad shit was happening, even when he played everything cool since losing a lot of his product.

"Lyric run, run. He has a gun," Lex yelled out. She never stopped her running speed towards me. I was still numb, lost in what the fuck to do in the moment. My mind couldn't register who had a gun or who the hell she was talking about. Everybody at the hangout was like family, while others were known around the block. They fought all the time around the way. I never saw someone pull out a gun though. My pop was supposed to have the streets on lock.

The sound of bullets firing across the distant made me snap back to reality. All I know was that one minute, I was on the phone with my pop, then Lex had my hand and we were running for our lives. People were scattering everywhere. I don't know where my friends went or if they were even okay. My mind couldn't think properly. I just knew I had to get the fuck away from the hangout before I was the next person lying in a casket for everybody to view and mourn. I wasn't going out like that. I refused to die at the hand of my pop's enemies when I had a whole life ahead of me.

"They dropped him, they fuckin' dropped him." Lex kept running. We ran all the way from the front of Eastside to Roberts St., where we lived. I swear it was like we were trying to win the gold medal in a Track & Field Olympics.

"Aye, y'all hop in." Osiris hit the brakes and his car skid to the left a bit, leaving tire marks on the blacktopped road.

I hopped in the front seat and Lex hopped in the back. Osiris pulled away before our doors were closed properly. He sped down the narrow roads like he'd lost his mind. The way he was acting, I knew shit was serious; I just didn't know how serious.

"Michael was just defending me and they gunned him down like a dog. Why they do that? Is it really that bad they have to harm people? I don't even know if he's dead or not. All I know was he told me to run and that's what I did. I should've never left him. I should've stayed beside him." Lex went to rambling on about what happened to her friend. She and Michael were tight like leggings on a big girl.

"Look, calm down. Let me think." Osiris sped past the stop sign like it wasn't even there. He hung a sharp right while he reached for his phone. "Boss, they're with me. Were you able to get Brier and Boni out the house before it went up?"

Time those words seeped from Osiris lips about my momma and Eboni, my body went numb again. I went most of my life living under my pop's protection. People were too afraid to mess with his family. They always had been. It seemed like the tables turned in under a week. The week before he was trying to find the niggas that blazed his warehouse, then the next they were after his family like we were some damn deer during hunting season. I kept praying that they were alright, that my pop would get all the enemies who were after his empire. The shit was hitting too close to home.

"I can't believe he's dead; he's dead. I can't believe this." Lex wailed in the backseat. I couldn't imagine going through that kind of pain; like losing a person close to me. Lex kept around a small crowd. Michael being her closest friend, he was cool people; I met him on a few occasions. He hung around a lot of people, and stayed out of the way. Never been in many fights, nor known to start any mess in the streets. His pop was a standoff kind of man. He practiced his faith like no other. He even preached to us a few times. "He had him killed."

"Calm damn, Lex. Just calm down. This is tough on everybody." With my body feeling numb, I managed to summon a reply. I would never sit up there and act like I understood the pain she was going through after losing Michael.

"I can't calm down. I can't. He's dead. He's deadddd," Lex screamed so loud, Osiris put the phone aside for a second to see what the hell was going on. I wished it were possible for me to dive to the back seat and hold her in my arms. Michael didn't deserve that fate and Lex wasn't deserving of that kind of pain.

"Just keep me updated. If I have to, I'll do a circle around and head that way. I'm taking the girls to HQ." Osiris focused on the conversation he was having over the phone. He was good at blocking things out and focusing on what he thought was important.

"He's dead." Lex said those words so many times, it sounded like she was chanting.

# BEATZ

T-Max told me it would be best to go ahead and put some more pressure on Don's crew by making a fake attempt at Lyric and Lex. That's the thing; it was supposed to be a fake hit to scare him a bit. To stir his crew up. My attack on Don's crew really put me on, had me looking like a boss amongst the 211s. But that day things went kind of left, and what was supposed to be a fake attempt turned into something more. My crew claimed to have gotten a lil' tight when Michael was trying to act like a tough guy, jumping in front of Lex. Thank God they did because they were 'bout to blast her away in hopes that it would show Don his reign was over.

"I said don't shoot. We weren't supposed to shoot, now we have somebody dead," I snapped once they were in the car. I left Ruffis and Jay to deal with Lex, and make her piss her pants a little while I went over to deal with Lyric. I was going to have one of the boys with me walk off in the middle of everybody chopping it up to shoot through the crowd, keeping our fingers crossed that nobody got hit, but nothing went as planned. Lex came running towards the hangout like she was about to lose her life, then I saw Ruffis chasing her across the concrete like a madman. I managed to call him off before he chased them up the street and gunned them down like animals.

"But that Eastside nigga was getting all tight like he was strapped or something. I don't know if you're aware, but the code is to shoot a nigga before they blast you," Ruffis said. He was nonchalant about the whole damn thing. He acted like murdering a kid wasn't a big deal. Our beef was with grown niggas, not kids who still had their whole life ahead of them.

"Nigga, shut the fuck up." I reached back across the seat and connected my Glock to Ruffis's face. I surprised myself with every stunt I pulled regarding the 211s. A few weeks ago, nobody could pay me to do the stuff I was doing. I looked down on niggas who waved guns around to instill fear in other people, and turned my nose up at the thought of shooting at innocent people. I changed. Changed in ways I wasn't proud of. It was too late for my redemption. "When I say no mutha-fuckin' bloodshed. I mean it."

"Aight." Ruffis managed to mumble a reply through busted lips and possibly cracked teeth. They were soon going to learn just how a square nigga got down.

"Good. Now the rest of you niggas know what's good. That kind of shit will not be tolerated. Let's stick to the real enemies." I spoke my peace and left it at that. Aside from having to deal with a mishap, I was only a few hours away from sitting in my first meeting with Wayne. Phons talked big back at the HQ like he knew Wayne would turn down my attempt to meet. However, Wayne accepted the meeting with open arms. He sounded pleased to hear from a member of the Alejos' family. He even spoke good words about the honchos before me.

I kicked Ruffis out the car before we reached the Southside, then me and the other members that tagged along for the day headed over to the Serge Gs' HQ. They were in Cedar Grove, about thirty-five minutes out from the Southside. They were city niggas while we were country thugs, but down to the root, we were all country; some just having the privilege of living in a city while others lived in a smaller town.

The parking lot was packed with exotic cars when we made it to the Serge Gs' HQ like they were in the middle of having a car show or were auctioning off cars. I knew how the Serge G crew was racking; I just didn't know how much paper they were bringing in until I saw the expensive things they owned.

I exited the car with my crew of three following my lead. It was supposed to be just T-Max and I in attendance, but T-Max made it clear that no honcho went any place without having guards protecting his life. Because when enemies struck, they were trying to kill. No in between.

"These all their cars?" I asked.

"Naw, that's all Wayne's cars. He bankrolls and he likes to show it," T-Max said. When we reached the front door, two men holding AK-47s stopped us. Wayne knew we were coming, so I couldn't understand why the fuck we were being stopped. He sounded straight when I spoke to him. What was the fuckin big deal?

*These niggas might blast me*, I thought with my heart beating faster than I wished. I was feeling bold all week, doing things out of the norm, but when I was face to face with niggas who looked like they were ruthless than any niggas I ever came across, it humbled me. I wasn't going to show any kind of fear, not in their presence. T-max had been putting me on game. He told me to never show fear to another man below my level or above.

"Up the weapons." The short, buff dude spoke. His voice was lighter than I assumed. Sounded like a nigga under his weight class.

"When have weapons ever been a problem?" T-Max spoke up in regards to their decision to confiscate our guns. They all were strapped.

"Not until today." The man viewed me with a smug look. It was easy to see that he had a problem with me. He didn't even know me from a can of paint. With his take on me, I knew he was referring to me as the problem.

"Alright, no problem. We'll hand them over and get them back after the meeting." I ordered my men to hand over the guns. We weren't there to cause problems, so putting the guns away wasn't a problem. I made sure we were complying with the rules of the Serge Gs until Wayne introduced me to everybody as the new honcho of 211 Vipers.

"Good choice." The man gave a sly smirk. Sooner than later he was going to learn to respect the new power on the throne, even if I had to get T-Max to knock his teeth down his throat on the low.

"Call the shots then," T-Max murmured as the men moved aside to let us in the Serge Gs' HQ. Theirs were fancier than ours. They had Santarelli chairs throughout the lobby, and a big sparkly chandelier hung in the center, making it look like the lobby of a five-star hotel. The floor was white marble with brown swirls. Whoever decorated the building had an excellent taste in décor.

"Oh, it's super dope in this joint." I had to give the props publicly. T-Max didn't say anything to my sudden outburst of appreciation of the place. I guess he was used to seeing things like that, but my feet were only getting wet.

* * *

Wayne was a smaller man than what I imagined, if he didn't have his body inked, he would've looked like any average man walking the streets. The ink made him look more hood, intimidating even. He sat behind the desk with his feet propped talking on the phone like he was two seconds away from putting steel in a nigga's ass.

"I don't give a flying fuck 'bout no other gang, we takin over territory. Shoot them niggas down. Can't have them slanging in our spot like that. We run his city." Wayne talked calmly. The way he said his words would make just about any man sweat. You couldn't tell he was upset by his words alone. I was told that men who kept their composure were the most violent. They were able to murder somebody with a straight face or even a smile. It's how they handled things. "Naw, it's cool. Just bust 'em. End of story."

"So, this the lil' nigga that's on the talk of everybody's lip." Wayne caught me off guard, because last I checked he was on the phone chopping it up with somebody, then all of a sudden, he was leaned back in the chair speaking to me.

"I don't know 'bout being on everybody's tongue." I reached out to shake his hand. It was said, *you are always able to test another man by the way he shakes your hand.* I was taught that by my uncle as a child. You found a man out by looking him straight in the eyes. A cutthroat nigga always talked with his head down. It's how they did things. I surprised myself with how much I knew about the hood, about street codes, and how to size up another man in his own establishment. I guess living in the hood taught a person that even if they weren't out there in the streets like everybody else.

"Well, if you ain't know, you will soon. I haven't been in an Alejos company in years. I forgot Cappo had other relatives out this way. You what? More black?" Wayne said.

"My mom's black, yeah. Alejos' blood runs through my veins from my dad's side. You know the seed follows the man." My words came out a bit nerdy. I stayed being technical with people, even when it wasn't called for.

"Uhm, I see. Another one of his brother's children." Wayne half turned his nose up at me.

"Another one of his brother's children?" I questioned.

"Yeah, you ain't know you and Gooch were brothers? Shiddd, Cappo always used to chop it up with me regarding personal things. Your old man was a rolling stone until his dying day." Wayne's eyes fell to T-Max then back to me in a split second. He leaned forward on the desk, his elbows keeping him propped. "But my question is, if your older brother was banished by Don for being in alliance with me, what makes you think he won't do the same to you?"

"I thought you and Cappo were enemies, like the 211s and Serge Gs were foes? I thought the gangs weren't in alliance until Gooch took over." I was speaking about what I knew.

"That's another story for a different day. Now answer my question," Wayne said.

I thought about my reply for a quick second, he had a good question. Don was good at offing niggas in the dark; taking their lives like a thief in the night. When I came after him, I knew he was going to come after me harder once he was found out. T-Max had no doubt that after the meeting with Wayne, my name was going to be on everybody's tongue.

"Well, I haven't thought that far ahead just yet. I'm still trying to figure out how to get him before he gets me. You know," I replied. The truth never hurt anyone to tell. Wayne knew I was new to the whole honcho thing, so I didn't see a problem being straight up with him.

"You know how many niggas tried to get Don over the years? It's good to just hate the man from a distance and respect him or just wait on him to off you," Wayne chuckled. T-Max cracked a chuckle too. I couldn't find anything funny. I was fed up with how much praise people gave Don and how he was in the middle of Lyric and I being together.

"I might just be the one who can get the job done, but I'm not here to talk 'bout all that. I'm here to let you know that my team appreciates you for looking out for them over the years, but I'm relinquishing them from under your wings; giving you a chance to breathe," I said.

"Giving me a chance to breathe?" Wayne raised his eyebrows. His ears perked up to my words.

"It's only right for me to take charge of the 211s. They're my responsibility now," I replied.

"You haven't been honcho for even a week now and you think you have the power to give them the guidance. Taking them from under my wings will only put you in a tight spot." Wayne viewed T-Max; his attention fell back to me again. "But as you wish." I figured he was taking my crew from under his wings easily because in his heart he probably felt like I was going to need him soon.

# OSIRIS

I never expected the next time I would see Lyric, would be under those kinds of circumstances. Don's enemies were growing like wildflowers, and those muthafuckas weren't a pretty sight either.

I couldn't even sit in the house with my Mom Duke that day to listen to the news she had regarding her test results. The moment she took a deep breath to lay it all on the table, Don called me and told me to go find Lyric and Lex. He made me swear I wouldn't let anything happen to them under my care. He told me somebody set his house on fire. I never heard so much panic in his voice until that day. It made me a bit uneasy myself. My nerves were shot. I knew if something happened to any of Don's family, he was going to go off on the deep end.

"Are they alright?" Lyric asked time we pulled into the parking lot of the HQ in Kingston. The building was off deep in the woods. The only people who were able to get up in there were niggas who were ranked high on the team like me. It was gated and surrounded by a big ass iron fence. It was the fuckin headquarters.

"Yeah, they are at the hospital now. Doctors trying to make sure they're straight after inhaling a lot of smoke." I let down the window to type the code in on the keypad at the gate. I watched the big gates slide open. On any other day, watching the gates open were therapeutic, but being in that moment, I was praying they hurry the fuck up just in case somebody followed us out there. The quicker I got Lyric and Lex behind the gates, the quicker the nerves in my stomach would settle.

"Can you please tell me who's after my family, Siris? I don't like this one bit. All this being in the dark." Lyric sounded like she was a second away from breaking down in tears.

"We're all in the dark, Lyric. Don't you think if we knew who was behind all of this, they would've been dropped days ago?" I parked the car up front, and hopped out before she was able to ask me any more questions. I wasn't in favor of playing twenty-one questions with her. There was too much mess going on out there on the streets for me to be answering questions that I didn't have the fuckin' answers to.

Gates was standing up front next to the entrance holding his Glock 19. 9mm, I swear I never saw that nigga with a different gun. Since Don demoted Gates a few years back and forced me to step up in the position, Gates kept away from the public. Word was he was too ashamed to show his face after Don humiliated him and made a joke of him to the other Warriors. But hell, I had my speculations. The code was to never trust a man that you underhand. And for Don's sake, I prayed he kept close tabs on Gates.

"What's up nigga?" I posted up next to Gates.

"Ain't nun." Gates kept his posture stiff. Gates had been with Don three years before I was initiated to the Warriors. I don't know what happened during those years to make Don see him through a different set of eyes, but it was either me taking the position or getting my ass murked out there. As a nigga of the streets, I knew better than to turn down a position that was given by an OG.

"You don't know who could be making hits like this. I mean, I did narrow it down to like three crews, but I still can't put my finger on why the fuck they would come for Don like that." I looked straight ahead, but I watched Gates from the corner of my eyes. He was always in the shadows.

"Nigga don't you think if I knew, you would know 'bout it now? Do it look like I'd keep some shit like that from the team?" Gates waved his gun around at me. The nigga seemed like he wanted to pop off. He had the wrong one, because as Don's right hand, I was able to make choices regarding nigga's lives on my own and deal with Don's wrath later. He was in favor of me; he let me slide with a little reckless shit from time to time.

"Aye homeboy, you on even want to go there with me. I asked you a damn question. Ain't no reason to be all big in the chest." I raised my White T up enough for him to see the black SIG P226 tucked in my waistband. The crew already knew how the fuck I was coming, so I don't know why Gates decided to speak to me without a lick of respect. "We straight on that?"

"Yeah, we good whoadie." Gates backed down off his high horse to see shit at my level. He already knew how I was coming. There was no room for muthafuckas to be getting tight with another nigga on the same team. Whoever was after Don was after us too. The streets worked that way. They punished niggas from association.

"Gates?" I looked over to the left of me. Lyric spoke his name like he was somebody special or some. Seeing him standing there seemed to lift her spirit.

"Lil' Lyric." Gates tucked the Glock away, and made his way over to Lyric like they were long lost lovers. They say eyes speak a thousand words; I think mine spoke like a million standing there watching them embrace each other. Gates was older than me by three years, and had Lyric beat by 'bout twelve. They couldn't have possibly had a thing for each other.

I watched him twirl her around then lower her to the ground. Out of all the years of knowing him, I never saw him crack a smile. He was big smiling with Lyric, showing all his iced-out teeth. It would've been petty of me to gun the man down like a dog for hugging up on Lyric.

"Where you been? I haven't saw you with Pops in forever." Lyric finally floated down from the excitement.

"I been around, just not in the spotlight like before. I like this better. I get to think." Gates spoke in a low tone like he didn't want anyone to hear his reply.

Right after he replied to Lyric, he turned his attention to Lex who was making her way up front. He met her halfway and picked her up like a knee-high child. I never been a jealous man, but I swear to see him being all friendly with them made my blood boil over. They were my family. I looked out for them solely. It was more than some job for me.

"Man, y'all are all grown up." Gates finally lowered Lex to the concrete. I had to dismiss myself from whatever they had going on. The facility was gated, the safest place they could be in the world. So, leaving them out there wasn't putting them in any kind of risk. Unless my gut wrenching feeling about Gates was right.

I entered the building with my chest a little high. They knew it was serious if I was there and Don wasn't. Whenever we swung by the headquarters, it was always together, but he was dealing with serious things now. He couldn't be there right away if he wanted.

"Look what the dog coughed up." Dre walked into the lobby with his AK hanging on a strap across his shoulder.

"What's up, bruh?" I gave Dre dab. He was the first to accept my dysfunctional ass on the team when Don introduced me to everybody. Most of them didn't like how he let me in without having to do all the shit they did to be on his team. I was just a young nigga back then; I was lost in the world. Grieving nothing but anger. Don saw through it and gave me a chance.

"Shidddd, staying on my toes like the rest. Don't know which way these niggas hitting from. I told Don, he should've offed the 211s years ago." Dre returned the dab. I heard a bit about the 211 Vipers over the years. Whatever beef Don had with them happened thirteen years ago. None of them bucked since. It happened three years before I got on. An older enemy was still an enemy though. Some crews took years to hash out a plan that would bring another man to his knees.

"What happened with that anyway? I mean, Don tells me a lot of shit, but old beef he doesn't seem to dwell on. It stays in the dark." I knew Dre wouldn't mind filling me in on old shit because he liked talking. Don almost knocked his jaw in one time when he was talking too much.

"Gooch traded sides; swore the 211s alliance to the rival gangs. Blackballed Don like it wasn't anything, so Don banished his ass from the streets. 211s still roamed the streets after Gooch banished; they never bucked though after that." Dre laid it out without really caring too much about the story.

"You don't think they're behind this?" Don's mind wasn't on it; mine was though. I dug up enemies that dated back to the nineties. He had a list of enemies who could've grown stronger and larger in number over the years while he was busy settling into a life he built for himself. The last five years, Don spent most of his time offering up peace offerings. He tried to get his foes count low, so he would be able to rest at night while Lyric rose to the throne. I had no doubt that she had the streets in her and could rule the Eastside Warriors, probably better than Don. However, it still didn't shake the fact that she was a woman. I couldn't count on one hand any women OGs out there; at least not in our state. Things were bound to go left at some point. We just had to make sure we were riding for Lyric when the time presented itself.

"Bruh, any nigga and his crew can be behind this. It could really be the 211 Vipers and Serge Gs behind this. Serge Gs have always been a big foe of Don, and since he offed Gooch, I know the 211s have it out for him. Wouldn't surprise me if those niggas teamed up over the years." Dre removed the AK from his shoulder and propped it against the sheet-glass walls. Word was Don liked to see everything going on, so the headquarters were mainly glass. He liked being on the first floor and able to see what was happening on the second. "I say we ride upon those niggas. Pay them a visit before they pay us one separately."

"Ride out on them, huh." I thought long and hard on that decision. Riding out on another gang had to be approved by Don. I ranked high on the crew, but there were still some rules I couldn't break. "I'll have to speak with Don on it; get his permission. You know how he gets about shit like that. He likes to keep the streets clean of gunplay."

"Well, you just let me know what's up. I'm ready to make that AK blast." Dre picked up the AK, tossing it back over his shoulder, and ditched me right in the lobby. I had to get in touch with Don, then hit up Jab to see what the fuck was taking so long with the footage. The day I brought the drive over to him to recover, it took us all damn night. The niggas he left on the porch had done drunk all his liquor and burnt out on his ass. Approaching three in the morning, I threw the towel in and told him to just hit me up if he found anything.

With my mind on one thing, I dialed Jab. "Bruh, tell me you found something."

"I don't know what those niggas did, but bruh I swear, I've tried every trick in the book to recover without an inch of luck." Defeat played in Jab's tone. I never knew him not to know what the fuck to do. He stayed recovering deleted shit. He was like one of those I.T. niggas without a badge. "I mean, they fucked it up, wiped it clean, slammed it, and broke it. Whatever the fuck they done, they did it good. Bruh, they had to have a good ass plan and an I.T. guy to pull this off."

Walking back and forward in the lobby, I replied, "That's not what I want to fuckin' hear. You sit at computers and shit all fuckin' day. You need to figure this out. Foes will come after everybody involved with us. I want to see you get out the hood, but if you don't come up with footage, you may suffer at their hand."

"I'll see what else I can do. You owe me, bruh. You fuckin' owe me." Jab ended the call before I was able to say anything else. I spoke the truth; I would never be able to stress enough that gangs came after people in association with rival gangs. It's how things went. There were statements that had to be made to make a honcho bow to the rival honcho's hand.

Right after I got off the line with Jab, I hit Don up to run some plans by him; possibly some leads too. Maybe the things Dre told me would jog his memory. "I know you're dealing wit—"

Don cut me off before I could even finish my sentence, "I'm heading over to headquarters. I'm calling an urgent meeting in the next hour." Then, before I was able to summon a reply, Don was no longer on the other end of the phone.

# LYRIC

Gates and Pop went way back. When I was a knee-high kid, I used to call him Uncle. Then, questioning my pop a few years later about what happened to Uncle Gates, he snatched my ass up and corrected me right away. He wasn't my damn uncle. I never opened my mouth about him being my uncle again. I never thought to question his whereabouts, although my mind sometimes fell on him.

"Alright listen up, the boss is on his way over here. He's going to be holding a mandatory meeting. I don't care if it's time for you to end your shift, you will stay until after the meeting. Understood?" Osiris stood front and center in the lobby, soaking in all the power he had by being my pop's right hand or whatever they called it. People would think, after being raised by honcho, I would know all there was to know about the streets. They were wrong though. When I was in school, my head stayed in the books, and I barely got into fights. I wanted different out of life.

"Stay around? We do that anyway, whoadie. Tell us something new. You think you're the only one who's dedicated the Warriors?"

I peeped since we first arrived how fly Gates was being with Osiris. I was too geeked to see him after all those years to intervene with whatever they had going on, or to even care about what they were discussing. But now that my mind was on what was happening to my family, to my Pop's team, Gates was stepping out of line speaking to Osiris that way. I didn't have to know much to know that Osiris was ranked high next to Pop. He was co-honcho to the Eastside Warriors, and he deserved more respect than what Gates was giving him.

"If you make one more smart remark while I'm speaking, I'm going to smash this SIG against your teeth" Osiris was firm when he replied to Gates, and Gates didn't speak another word after Osiris said what he had to say. The hour everybody waited on Pop was long and tiresome. He had guards at the hospital with momma and Boni, while he headed over to headquarters to make sure his crew was in line.

"Does anybody else have something to say to me? Speak up or forever hold your muthafuckin' peace." Osiris looked around the room waiting for somebody to speak up. I couldn't blame them for keeping their mouth closed. He was strapped, and with being a right hand, he would shoot them without paying any kind of consequences.

"Naw, you good bruh. We all on the same page." A short, baldheaded man replied. I believe Osiris called him by some name that starts with a D.

"Alright Dre, make sure you make another sweep of the building. The only people that's not expected to be in attendance is the niggas that work the cameras." Osiris spoke to the short, baldheaded man. The crumbly nigga that I then knew as Dre. He ran to the drop of Osiris's commands. As long as I been alive, that's the closest I ever got to my pop's team. It was crazy how one man held so much power. I imagined myself being in those same shoes, having niggas bowing to me, and running around the building at the mention of my name, but I blocked it out quick as it arrived. I didn't need those kinds of thoughts poisoning my mind. I had to stay focused on what I wanted out of life. The true legacy that I wanted my own name to carry. One that didn't involve murdering people, forcing their families to bury them six feet under.

"Did you get the shipment to the border, Oakdog?" Osiris looked at the tall, fair-skinned man that stood to the left of Gates. He had to be no more than twenty, hell, probably wasn't even that. When Osiris spoke, his ears perked up to the words. I never saw how much power Osiris had until I witnessed it. I underestimated him big time. He wasn't just some man that was up my pop's ass; he was running things too.

"Yeah, all that is taken care of. I didn't run into any problems either. Went smoother than I thought it would," Oakdog replied with his hands resting behind his back like he was in the Marines. I knew my pop was big out there in the drug game, but I wasn't aware that his team was smuggling shit across borders.

"Good, keep that up. Greater things are in store for you." Osiris showed his appreciation for Oakdog. The whole time they were chopping it up, Lex was glued to her pain like the world was snatched from underneath her feet. Since we been at the headquarters, she hadn't opened her mouth to say much, and had I been in her shoes, I probably would've been the same way. She lost a good friend.

"Already," Oakdog replied with his arms still behind his back. I saw it then; a person just had to show respect to a man like Osiris. He was younger than most people in the gang when he got promoted as my pop's right hand. I heard the stories on the streets about him, which made me like him more now. I think part of me was pulling toward him because he showed up out the blue, and scooped us up when people were after us. I know I didn't owe him for doing his job, it felt like I did though.

"You straight?" Osiris almost made me jump into a new body. I was too busy observing things to see him approach me. The last I saw him, he was standing in the middle of everybody getting them in line.

"Fuck! You scared me." I placed my left hand over my chest like that would calm my nerves. Instant embarrassment shot through my body when all eyes fell on me.

"Scared you? You was looking right at me the whole time I was walking over to you." Osiris widened his eyes at me like I'd lost my mind. That's what it felt like too. Like I lost my entire damn mind.

"I was zoned out. In my thoughts is all," I replied. My voice was a whisper in the back of my throat.

"You good though? I mean, are y'all good?" Osiris asked, turning his attention from me to Lex. She was too glued to her phone to even reply. I could only imagine what social media was saying about her friend's death. I could just about place my finger on the fact that it was already a headline in town. Mansfield was small and news traveled like wildfire.

"I just want my momma 'em to be straight. That's all my mind can think about right now." I lowered my head. Tears tickled my eyes. The flood of emotions ran up my throat, and for a split second, I thought I was about to lose it in front of all those people. And just when my lips started trembling and the tears were on the verge, Pop walked through the doors and took the attention and pressure away from me.

"There he is." Osiris walked over to Pop like God graced the doors of the HQ, and in acknowledgement of his presence, all the Warriors placed their hands behind their back in respect of him.

"Where's Dre?" Pop asked time he walked in the building. It was at least a hundred men standing in the lobby. For him to know one was missing let me know right away, that he was on his shit. He knew when one person was missing out of a hundred; that was insanely observant of him.

"He'll be back down in a few. I sent him to do a sweep of the building and to make sure the other niggas are watching the cameras." Osiris shot his reply without a crack in his tone. Anybody could tell how close he was with Pop. He spoke to him like he was just another nigga in the room. Osiris never had to speed with his words or move around like he lost his mind. It was the position he held that kept him composed.

"Alright. While we wait on him, I need to check out a few things." Pop moved past Osiris. He looked over at Lex and I, then turned his attention straight ahead to where Gates stood. "You wasn't going to tell me you had a run-in with one of the Serge Gs a month ago? What kind of fuck shit is that?"

"It wasn't a run in with nobody. They saw me, I saw them and that was it. We didn't even pass any words. We were in passing." Gates spoke those words like he had a monkey on his back. I bucked my eyes at the way he spoke to Pop. I never saw it with my own eyes, but I heard what he did to men who tried to disrespect him. Word was that my pop was colder than any nigga to ever walk the street.

"Don't you think that's something I still should know? When do you ever just run into Serge Gs? They keep low, low profiles. Blend in with the general population. So, if you saw one, they wanted to be seen for a reason. Shouldn't you know this by now? You been with the team what, thirteen years? And you still don't know shit." Pop grabbed a pistol from his waistband while his walking pace didn't let up. I knew he was pressed from way across the room, because when he spoke those words, his voice bounced off the walls like the roar of a lion.

"I..." Gates backed down from his reply once Pop took up the space in front of him. I lowered my eyes for a moment, praying like hell I didn't have to witness Gates get his brain blew back.

"You what nigga?" Pop raised his voice louder than the first time. I was shaking in my shoes, so I knew Gates was a second away from pissing his pants if he had an ounce of fear for my pop's rage.

"I should've told you. It's just been so long since we had any problems with them, I didn't suspect anything." Gates kept his head straight with his hands behind his back. I don't know how Pop put fear in those men's heart, but it was there and wasn't going anywhere. He was that muthafuckin' nigga.

"I should pop a hole right through your head. And you wonder why a young nigga took your spot. I took you under my wings after you proved yourself worthy, then you turned out to be one big ass charity case." Pop aimed the gun at Gates' forehead. I closed my eyes for a second, paying again that he spared Gate's life. He had just been happy to see Lex and I after all those years of not being able to, now we were standing there in witness of him being humiliated.

"I ain't mean no harm, whoadie. I swear it on my life." Gates' face turned red like Cayenne. He was a light man, so it didn't take much to see the blood flourish to his face.

"You meant harm if you keep your team in the dark on shit like that. This ain't over, and that's on my life." Pop lowered the gun, giving me a moment to breathe in the thin, crisp air. My lungs felt damaged from all the anxiety that crept from my chest to my back. My nerves were on edge.

"Ayeeee, boss." Dre walked from downstairs into the lobby in high spirit. I wished somebody had given him the memo to cut that shit. Pop wasn't playing with niggas that evening.

"Quiet that bullshit and fall in line," Pop shouted out more demands. He was bossing people around like his life depended on it.

# OSIRIS

I waited out in the car with Lyric and Lex while Don wrapped up with the last of his conversation with the rest of the Warriors. I was waiting for him to give me the rest of the plan. Like where the hell he wanted me to take Lyric and Lex since somebody burned down the house. They could've stayed with me, but since the hood was in an uproar, the last thing we needed was for them to be back on that side of the trenches. Not until things cooled down out there. People were out for their blood so they could teach Don a lesson. From what I knew about the Serge Gs, they murdered children in the streets without pity. When they sent a message, they really were set on sending a damn message.

"You seem upset," Lyric spoke after being in the car for ten minutes. Lex was already in the backseat sound asleep. She had a rough day, and deserved to get some rest. I expected Lyric to be out cold too, but she was still up trying to see what was up.

"Naw, I'm just on high alert. Between looking out for y'all and dealing with my Mom Duke's situation, it puts a strain on a nigga." I beat around the bush 'bout Mom Duke's health problems without directly telling Lyric something was wrong with her. I hadn't really opened up about anything concerning my life to anyone. I had to be strong. It was my persona.

"What's wrong with Ms. Vi?" Lyric focused on the last of my sentence more than I hoped. She had that about her; she focused on the small details of the information that was given to her.

"I-she, well I don't really know yet. I had to run to save the day when she was 'bout to share the test results with me. She believes its breast cancer, last stage that is." I wouldn't allow myself to focus on my words for too long. The reality was setting in quicker than before, and it really hit me that my Mom Duke probably wouldn't live to see the next holiday if the doctors didn't work some kind of miracle.

"So, you left her in the cold like that to come running to our side? Siris, I know it's not my place, but you should be there for you momma. I can talk to my pop, tell him something came up and you had to dip. You need to be there for her," Lyric replied with the deepest sympathy a woman could give a man. Her words sent chills down my spine, and made me feel crippled from the waist up. I fucked around with plenty of women in the past, but none of them cared enough to give me advice or try to help me ease the pain like Lyric. She was willing to face Don on my behalf. I couldn't accept that.

"She's gon' be fine. She knows how deep this goes. I knew what I signed up for when Don took me under his wings. You can't leave your team hanging when enemies hit the fan. That's code." I hopped out the car when I saw Don walking out of the building. It took me a good ten seconds to close the air space that lied between us.

"Take them to a hotel in Shreveport. I'm going back down to the hospital with Brier and Boni. They're keeping them overnight. I'm more than certain nobody knows where Lyric and Lex are going, so I'm not worried about that." Don looked past me with his eyes focused on my car. "You promise me that no matter what happens you will look out for them with your own life?"

"I gotcha, boss. You don't have to worry 'bout a thing." I nearly choked on my own words as they seeped from my throat. Don's words hit me in places that they never touched before. It almost sounded like he was giving up, or maybe he was feeling something. I didn't want it to be so. Don and the Eastside Warriors always came out on top. It was our thing. No nigga ever crossed us bad enough for us to bow or lose our hand in the gang. We were feared men throughout the states, and Don was the muthafuckin' honcho that most niggas died to be like. He paved the way for niggas who never had a chance out there in the world.

"Don't let me down." Don ended the conversation and headed over to his black on black Tahoe. Axe was waiting with the door open. Normally it would be Don and I rolling around the city on a mission. I still held the same position, but the tables had turned, and he had me protecting his girls while he relied on a man he barely trusted with his life. Axe was new to the team, only a year deep and was rolling with the boss, soaking up all the good grace.

* * *

I believe it was around three o'clock in the morning when I rolled over to see Lyric staring up into the ceiling. Don made sure he booked one of the fanciest hotels in downtown Shreveport. It had two bedrooms along with two separate baths, a living room and dining area. He wanted them to feel like they were at home. Originally, I chose to sleep on the couch in the living room, however, Lyric claimed she couldn't sleep and would feel safe if I was in the room with her.

"Why you still up?" I asked.

"I could ask you the same?" Lyric said those words without turning to look my way. The streaks of light that shined through the drapes made her look breathtaking. With all we both were going through, it was wrong for those thoughts to be going through my mind, but I couldn't help myself. Lyric had a way of taking a nigga's heart and grabbing him in for life.

"I'm sorry this is happening right now. I wish I could find the gang responsible for this, and make them pay for crossing the Eastside Warriors; your family specifically." I was staring at her side profile as I said those words. My dick stood up in that bed, betraying the innocent moment that lied between us. "We gon' get them."

"How are you going to do that if you're busy trying to protect us?" Lyric finally turned around in bed. She viewed me with the sexiest bedroom eyes. Don gave me permission to be with her, but it felt off limits then. We were dealing with some serious threats against the gang; didn't know which niggas were hitting or why the fuck they decided to be private enemies number one.

"I can do anything and everything babe. I'm overly qualified," I said.

"Anything?" Lyric's voice was a whisper. With the way she was looking at me and how her voice sounded, there was no doubt she was referring to sex. Don kept a tight leash on his daughters. I suspected she was a virgin, and breaking her virginity wasn't fit for a night like that.

"Yeah anything," I flirted back, knowing it wasn't the right thing to do. Don trusted me to protect them, to look out for them while we were at the hotel. Not to get into bed with her, and spoil her innocence. Not too long after I said those words, Lyric climbed on top of me. She leaned forward, her hair getting in the way of the view, kissed my lips and grinded her hips against my rock-hard dick like she'd drunk way too much liquor and it gave her the confidence to do what she been wanting to do.

"Don't worry, this ain't my first time." Lyric's words resembled a woman beyond her age.

"Good girl ain't really that good, I see." I snaked my tongue in her mouth. Her lips were plump; the nicest pair of lips I saw on a woman. Part of me was jealous to know another man fucked her before me, and the fact that any man messed around with her in the first place. She was supposed to be the well-behaved woman that was the princess of the block. I had been under the impression that Don placed his fear in her to not be stupid like the other girls in the hood.

"They say good girls are the worse ones." Lyric reached her hand below my waist, and removed my dick from the shorts, on a mission to have me inside of her. Since last year, all I was able to think about was her reaching the age that she was old enough to let me have her. However, another nigga beat me to the line. It was crazy to even be thinking like that while she was on top of me, but I couldn't stop myself from wondering who she'd been with.

"I guess I know that as the truth now," I murmured through the kisses while I held her hips. She positioned herself over my dick and slid down like the pro she sought out to prove herself to be.

"Hmmm, it's so big," Lyric moaned out as she rode my dick like a cowgirl. I slept with a lot of women throughout my life, but none of them compared to what I was feeling being inside of Lyric that morning. Her pussy was tight and equipped for the ride. It pissed me off whenever I heard men say all pussy was the same. That was a bold ass lie. Some bitches had pussy that could fit ten niggas inside, plus a set of hands. Lyric didn't fit into that batch; she was still tight and barely broken in.

"You like that?" I held her still and pounded into her with quick, deep strokes. If she was really going to be with me, she had to learn quickly that I liked being in control, not the other way around. I was an alpha male, and hardly ever liked a woman being an alpha female. Being a man in all situations was adrenaline that only I was able to understand.

"Ohhh, fuck! Shit that feels so good. Don't stop, don't stop." Lyric's moans and words were rising higher and higher with each stroke. Waking Lex wasn't a good idea, so I placed my hand over her mouth to muffle her screams. Under different circumstances I enjoyed a screamer, but not when a woman's little sister was in the other room grieving a terrible loss.

"You gon' have to keep it down. Keep it down." I removed my hand from over her mouth after a while.

"Okay," Lyric whispered. I picked her up, and flipped her over onto her back. I wanted her to feel all of me and I couldn't force her to feel it with her being on top. I was in need of pounding into her pussy, in an attempt to reach her guts. She was going to feel me for a week, even if we didn't mess around again during that same week.

"Now feel me," I groaned.

"Ouuu," Lyric moaned. Her moans were an instant intoxication, suddenly taking me into the trenches. I stroked her with passion, with intensity. Each stroke brought her closer to me; our bodies getting to know each other.

"Hold your legs," I directed, letting her know exactly how I liked it. My mission was to please her, and to show her how to please me too, because if she was going to be my woman, exclusively, she had to know how to send my body to the climax.

"Ouuu, Siris. Oh my God, it feels so good. It feels sooo good." Lyric raised her voice again, sending chills over my body. I no longer cared about who heard her or how wrong it was sexing her body when there was somebody after her family. My mind wouldn't allow me to dwell on anything other than that moment with Lyric.

# BEATZ

"I haven't been seeing you in the studio much." Momma stopped me in the hallway with her words. My mind was working in overtime on what to say to her. I mean, she would've believed if I said it was frustration for not getting enough recognition or maybe if I even told her that Pooh and I had a terrible breakup.

"Yeah, can't really think 'bout music right now. Pooh and I broke up not long ago. She was my heart, and losing her from my life really hurts." Standing there in the hallway, I forgot the code I was taught. *Never drop your head when you're telling a lie.* My momma knew me better than anyone. I had girlfriends in the past, and she was aware of how I dealt with things after breakups. I usually channeled all my anger towards music. It was my only escape; the only thing that allowed me to speak without it talking back.

"Why you telling a tale? Did I raise you to lie to me? You best fess up to what you have going on. People been telling me things, I just need to hear it from my son." Momma placed her hands on her hips. She wasn't known to back down when she demanded answers.

"What are you talking 'bout, Ma?" I tried to act as clueless as a drunk man on a Friday night at the club.

"You let T-Max and those animals swindle you into joining a bullshit gang. You graduated high school, have the best transcript to get into a good college, and you have talent. I didn't think I raised a boy dumb enough for some lowlifes to get in his head and persuade him to throw his life away for the streets." I saw tears well in Momma's eyes, but they weren't sad tears. The way rage filled her eyes, I knew she was one sentence away from knocking me back to the Sunday before.

"Can you hear me out?" I asked.

"Hear you out? No, you hear me the fuck out. You gon' take your ass over there and tell T-Max you're out the gang. I don't mind calling the police to bust his old washed up ass. He or nobody will be the reason I lose my son due to gang violence, gunplay in a bloodbath or whatever the hell. I've been a witness too many times to young black men losing their lives early because of foolish and bad company." Momma snapped on me like I was ten years old again. She had to understand, I was grown now, not some lil' boy she could push around and straighten out. I was in too deep now to fold on the 211 Vipers. They probably would've murdered me in cold blood if I ran for the hills.

"It's not that simple. I can't turn my back on them now. I have Alejo blood running through my veins. Uncle Cappo sealed our family name on that throne. It was meant for me to grow up and fulfill his duties. Take pride in his legacy," I said.

Momma reached out and slapped me so hard, I thought I heard thunder after the strike! "You will not live in my house as long as you're a part of that gang. I will not have trouble at my doors on account of anybody. I work hard, mind my business, and don't bother anybody. If that's the life you choose for yourself then so be it, but I want you gone by sunrise." She walked away without saying another word. My conscience wouldn't let me feel bad about my decision. I went most of my life being good to be people, looking out for them before I looked out for myself with little to nothing in return. Those same people weren't there whenever I needed them, and I was forced to deal with whatever problems I was facing alone. I slid my momma's words right out my ears, but if she wanted me gone then I was going to be gone. There was no doubt in my mind that she was going to come back around to accept my decision.

It had to be around twelve o'clock midnight; I called Lyric a few times only for the voicemail to answer every time. I left a few messages, trying to see if she was alright. Just trying to be there for her although I was the cause of whatever pain she was going through. None of it was done to hurt her; I was set on cleaning the path that was hindering us both. Then in the end, I was hoping she liked the new me, the nigga who no longer cared about trying to be perfect or appearing uptight to people in passing.

Aye. Big head. I know we ain't on the best of terms, but I just want to know if everything is alright. I'm worried. I read the text message a million times before pressing send. I felt strange playing both parts. Lyric and I had been honest with each other since we were children, now I was in the middle, trying to disguise myself in some damn sheep's clothing. When the time was right, I had to see Lex too, and let her know how sorry I was for her loss. Everybody on the block knew how close she and Michael were. They were damn near conjoined at the hips. Michael ain't never harm nobody either. But damn I stood at the head of those orders; the orders that resulted in his death. The blood was on my hands, although I didn't pull the trigger.

Hey, I'm cool. I read Lyric's message with a bitter taste in my mouth. Her reply was dryer than the sand in New Mexico. So dry that I imagined trails of dust.

Where ya at? I want to see you to be sho'. I sent the text without rereading it. I prayed like hell she told me where she was at and if it was possible for me to swing by. We were at war with each other, literally at war. I had to see her before she found at what was really going on; before Osiris got wind of anything and ratted me out.

The reply bubble popped up on the screen, so I knew she was typing. About three seconds later, they vanished. I saw them again and they went away. I contemplated sending another text to speed up her reply. My nerves were shot at the thought of her already knowing I was honcho of the 211 Vipers. If she found out, I would've liked it to be on my own time; like really talk it through with her.

After waiting for thirty minutes for her to reply, I finally put the phone away. Since my momma had already kicked me out for not making the decision that was in her favor, I packed a few of my things that would get me by for like a week, then I was going to head back over to get the rest. Moving out meant I was forced to make ends meet on my own, and find a new space to do my music if I ever returned to my roots.

* * *

"It ain't nothing you can't get up from. This ain't going to knock you down." T-Max walked beside me. The main office was supposed to be strictly for conducting business, but it was going to be used for my bedroom and the office.

"I'm not sweating it. I knew what I was getting myself into from jump," I replied like nothing bothered me. Yeah, I knew what kind of struggle it was going to be, to a certain degree, but I wasn't expecting to be thrown out and have my momma turn her back on me. I understood where she was coming from. Harm coming to her door on my account wasn't something I was going to live down.

"You ain't got to act all tough 'round me. I know what you goin' through. I went through the shit like forever and a day ago, but I still know how it feels. It's hard when your family turns on you because you want to be loyal to a gang. Count you out because you get your bread a way that's frowned upon. You just have to work your ass off now and ball on them later. Buy your momma a car or some shit down the road." T-Max handed me a spare set of keys to the building and left me alone. It was going to take time to get used to living on my own, caring for myself every step of the way. However, I knew I had the skills to make it through it.

*I can't believe this is my life right now*; I thought as I opened the office door and let myself inside. The office was dope; it wasn't like I was living in some shotgun house. Still, it was a change.

I'm downtown Shreveport at the Horseshoe. Lyric's text caught me completely by surprise. I was going to be heading to see her very soon, regardless if niggas found me out or not.

# LYRIC

"You let him know where you at? I thought we made it clear that nobody is to be trusted," Osiris said out of nowhere after he read the message Beatz sent me earlier in the morning. I knew he and I were messing around, but he didn't have any damn right to be reading a damn thing on my phone. Besides, Beatz was my friend, kind of like my boyfriend. I knew Beatz longer than Osiris.

"You goin' through my phone already?" I folded my arms, and positioned all my weight to one leg. He had me fucked up. "You need to understand that Beatz is my friend. He has a right to know where I am and how I'm doing."

Osiris paced the room like he had a chip on his back; he wasn't fond of Beatz since day one. Even the damn night he saw me out with him, he had something to say like Beatz was a soft nigga and couldn't protect me. He had it sealed in his mind that only a true hood nigga was able to protect me and keep me out of harm's way.

"Have you learned anything from Don? Friends are bigger enemies than distant enemies. You have friends who cut your throat every damn day." Osiris stopped moving altogether. He viewed me with an expression of disappointment.

"Beatz isn't like that. Can you just calm down? Give me some space," I argued.

"I'm calm. This is the calmest you ever gon' see me, but I'm not letting you go out there with him alone. Or go anywhere, for that matter. That nigga has Alejos' blood flowing through his veins, and we don't know who's after Don or wants him to fall by the wayside, so we gon' be on high alert from here on out," Osiris said.

I rolled my eyes at Osiris's words. What we shared in the wee hours was something special, and I was stuck on him for it, but he wasn't going to cripple me like that. It irked my soul to see a nigga get pressed about another nigga because they weren't secure enough in their own position with their girl.

"Whatever." I moved past Osiris in utter disgust. He worked my last nerve. With all the drama that was going on, Beatz and my situationship was suffering, hell I even betrayed him in more ways than I was okay to mention. He was there for me more than anybody outside of my family, and I kept him close through a lot of things.

Lex was standing at the window in the living room viewing the city skyline when I walked in. When we made it to the hotel the night before. She didn't speak a whole lot. I didn't expect her to though. She was going through something that nobody but her was able to understand.

"You straight?" I asked, knowing the answer already. Lex was a very private person when it came down to her going through things. She kept to herself most of the time, but she found it in her to vent to me when she built up her nerves.

"Uh, is that even a real question? I just think it's funny how Michael gets dropped time I decide to retaliate against Pop." Judging from

Lex's words, she had Pop ruled out as the bad guy. He was ruthless as ever, but to pin something like that on him was ridiculous.

"So, you think this whole grandiose thing has something to do with you? Like Pop would pull all this to teach you a lesson?" I shook my head because people were losing their minds and being ridiculous that morning; starting with Osiris reading my messages to Beatz. "I know you two are at odds, but blaming him is too much. We almost lost Momma and Eboni, that's enough within itself."

"You always taking up for him, regardless of what he do. You can talk all that big shit when you mad, but at the end of the day you defend him in every way possible." Lex argued with me like I was the enemy.

"I'm not doing this right now. You're hurting, so you're finding comfort in lashing out at everyone, but I'm not your enemy." With those words, I left her in the living room to deal with her grief alone for a while.

I'm 'bout to pull up now. Be outside. I read Beatz's message before sliding my phone into my back pocket.

I let myself out the room as quick as I could. Osiris was persistent on being out there with me when I met with Beatz, but I didn't want him out there in our presence. Beatz and I had something to discuss; personal issues. I learned about his breakup with Pooh through the grapevine. Normally, he would've called me up or told me to come over to discuss what he was going through, but he was still mad, madder than I ever witnessed. He was holding a grudge over my head, which made me thankful to see that he wanted to know if I was alright or not.

When I was down in the lobby, I received another text from Beatz. He told me he was pulling up in an all-black Monte Carlo. When I saw the car pull up to the front entrance near the valet parking, who he was riding with was a big question in my mind.

"You alright?" Beatz said time he hopped out the car. He met me at the doors before I was able to meet up with him at the car.

"Yeah I'm making it," I said. My heart was beating with anxiety that Osiris was going to come down and cause a scene.

"Damn, I hate that happened to y'all. It made me realize how short life really is and how bad things take only a second to happen," he replied.

In the middle of talking to Beatz, my pop pulled up in his black on black Tahoe. I wasn't expecting to see him so soon with all he had going on.

"Get down." I heard Osiris's voice blast from the back of me and seconds later bullets started rippling. I laid flat on the concrete praying like hell a bullet didn't hit me or the three people I care about.

*Please God, make it stop...*

# NOTE FROM AUTHOR K.A. WILLIAMS

Thank you for your continued support. I hope I was able to fulfill your literary cravings like usual. Part 2 will be releasing soon, so be on the lookout.

To stay in the loop with what I'm working on and all of my nail-biting short stories, please follow me on my social media accounts below.

**Facebook: Author K.A. Williams**

**Facebook Group: K.A. Williams' Beauties**

**Twitter: @kawilliams_**

**Instagram: @k.a._williams**

# ABOUT THE AUTHOR

K.A. Williams is an Urban Romance author signed with Royalty Publishing House. She also published Historical Fiction novels under her company Storytellers Publication, allowing her to express her passion for African American history while at the same time putting glamour on Urban life.

K.A. Williams made her debut in the literary industry back in 2012 at only sixteen years old with the release of *The Forbidden Truth* and *Jake's Lineage* short story trilogy. K.A. Williams has written over twenty books over the span of five years.

K.A. Williams is also a screenplay writer, adapting her novel *Jake's Lineage* into a movie with pending casting dates.

K.A. Williams resides in Mansfield, Louisiana with her husband and daughter.

**Stay Connected:**
**Facebook Group: K.A. Williams' Readers Circle**

facebook.com/AuthorK.A.Williams
twitter.com/kawilliams_
instagram.com/k.a._williams

## OTHER BOOKS BY THE AUTHOR

Dirty Secrets & Broken Bottles

Falling Hard for a Savage 1-3

Lovin' A Thug Till My Last Breath

Intoxicated by Hood Love 1-4

Falling for His Savage Love 1-3

Lovin' The Godfather of the Streets 1-3

Lovin' A Jamaican Godfather

Massa's Baby

Fragments of Autumn

Jake's Lineage

Afterlife

Dolly and Moe

CPSIA information can be obtained
at www.ICGtesting.com
Printed in the USA
LVHW031736290719
625730LV00004B/851

9 781077 830509

**Royalty Publishing House** is now accepting manuscripts from aspiring or experienced urban romance authors!

**WHAT MAY PLACE YOU ABOVE THE REST:**

Heroes who are the ultimate book bae: strong-willed, maybe a little rough around the edges but willing to risk it all for the woman he loves.

Heroines who are the ultimate match: the girl next door type, not perfect - has her faults but is still a decent person. One who is willing to risk it all for the man she loves.

The rest is up to you! Just be creative, think out of the box, keep it sexy and intriguing!

If you'd like to join the Royal family, send us the first 15K words (60 pages) of your completed manuscript to submissions@royaltypublishinghouse.com